Freeman Wills Crofts was [...] died in 1957. He worked f[or ...] company as an engineer until 1929, before turning to detective fiction.

His plots reveal his mathematical training and he specialised in the seemingly unbreakable alibi and the intricacies of railway timetables. He also loved ships and trains and they feature in many of his stories.

Crofts' best-known character is Inspector Joseph French. French appears for the first time in *Inspector French's Greatest Case*. He is a detective who achieves his results through dogged persistence.

Raymond Chandler praised Crofts' plots, calling him 'the soundest builder of them all'.

BY THE SAME AUTHOR
ALL PUBLISHED BY HOUSE OF STRATUS

THE 12.30 FROM CROYDON
THE AFFAIR AT LITTLE WOKEHAM
ANTIDOTE TO VENOM
THE BOX OFFICE MURDERS
THE CASK
CRIME AT GUILDFORD
DEATH OF A TRAIN
DEATH ON THE WAY
ENEMY UNSEEN
THE END OF ANDREW HARRISON
FATAL VENTURE
FEAR COMES TO CHALFONT
FOUND FLOATING
FRENCH STRIKES OIL
GOLDEN ASHES
THE GROOTE PARK MURDER
THE HOG'S BACK MYSTERY
INSPECTOR FRENCH AND THE CHEYNE MYSTERY
INSPECTOR FRENCH AND THE STARVEL TRAGEDY
INSPECTOR FRENCH'S GREATEST CASE
JAMES TARRANT, ADVENTURER
A LOSING GAME
THE LOSS OF THE JANE VOSPER
MAN OVERBOARD!
MANY A SLIP
MYSTERY IN THE CHANNEL
MURDERERS MAKE MISTAKES
MYSTERY OF THE SLEEPING CAR EXPRESS
MYSTERY ON SOUTHAMPTON WATER
THE PIT-PROP SYNDICATE
THE PONSON CASE
THE SEA MYSTERY
SILENCE FOR THE MURDERER
SIR JOHN MAGILL'S LAST JOURNEY
SUDDEN DEATH

FREEMAN WILLS CROFTS

Anything to Declare?

Copyright by the Society of Authors

All rights reserved. No part of this publication may be reproduced, stored in a retrieval system, or transmitted, in any form, or by any means (electronic, mechanical, photocopying, recording, or otherwise), without the prior permission of the publisher. Any person who does any unauthorised act in relation to this publication may be liable to criminal prosecution and civil claims for damages.

The right of Freeman Wills Crofts to be identified as the author of this work has been asserted in accordance with sections 77 and 78 of the Copyright, Designs and Patents Act 1988.

This edition published in 2000 by House of Stratus, an imprint of Stratus Holdings plc, 24c Old Burlington Street, London, W1X 1RL, UK.

www.houseofstratus.com

Typeset, printed and bound by House of Stratus.

A catalogue record for this book is available from the British Library.

ISBN 1-84232-382-2

This book is sold subject to the condition that it shall not be lent, resold, hired out, or otherwise circulated without the publisher's express prior consent in any form of binding, or cover, other than the original as herein published and without a similar condition being imposed on any subsequent purchaser, or bona fide possessor.

This is a fictional work and all characters are drawn from the author's imagination. Any resemblance or similarities are entirely coincidental.

CONTENTS

PART 1: THE BITERS BITE

1	THE SCHEME	3
2	THE PREPARATIONS	23
3	THE FIRST TRIP	38
4	THE MARSHAM EXPEDITION	55
5	THE CHINK IN THE ARMOUR	75
6	THE SURE WINNER	87
7	THE COUNTER BLAST	99
8	THE SETTLEMENT	119

PART 2: THE BITERS BIT

9	THE CALL TO FRENCH	139
10	THE RAMSGATE PASSENGER	152
11	THE CIVILIAN COLLEAGUE	166
12	THE MULTIPLE ARRESTS	179
13	THE MISSING LINK	195
14	THE CROWNING ITEM	207

PART 1

The Biters Bite

– 1 –

THE SCHEME

As Peter Edgley strode for the last time down the office stairs and out into the street, the wave of furious exaltation which had supported him during the last trying ten minutes began to ebb. It had been a great moment when after months of irksome restrictions and petty slights, of humiliations and growing resentment, he had let himself go and told his chief exactly what he thought of him. Incredible the sense of relief it gave him when just for once he had answered back, giving as good, and more than as good, as he had got! Surprised, the old blighter had been too. He had goggled and gaped like a fish as he had listened to remarks which he hadn't believed a man in his position could ever have heard.

A great moment, yes; but short lived. Edgley had of course been dismissed and already the revulsion of feeling was setting in, leaving him cold and flat. He had lost a job, and even in these days of full employment that was no light matter. Once again, as so often in the past, his unruly temper had got the better of him, and with the usual disastrous result. Except for the momentary gratification, never once had he gained anything but regrets from his outbreaks.

ANYTHING TO DECLARE?

Peter Edgley had perhaps found it harder than most to settle down once again in civilian life. An ex-commando and paratroop officer, he had seen thrilling service in many lands. He had shown impressive courage and had developed unexpected qualities of leadership and resource. He had been beloved by his men and trusted by his superiors. Though he had not received any special decoration, those with whom he had served believed that he deserved it more than many who had.

To come back from this large living to the rather junior occupation of costing quantities for a firm of builders was for him a bitter anticlimax. But he was painstaking and industrious and would have done the work, and done it well, had it not been for the atmosphere of the office. His departmental chief! He was the snag. To be treated as a rather helpless child, unable to deal with the simplest matters on his own responsibility, was galling in the extreme. The manager on his part was a weak man both physically and morally. He felt dwarfed and humiliated by his forceful subordinate, and in an unconscious attempt to repair his injured self-esteem, tended to throw his weight about. For some time both men had felt that a trifle only would be needed to bring matters between them to a head.

That afternoon the trifle had materialized. Approaching quitting time Scholes' buzzer had sounded: three pips, which was for Edgley. It was seldom for anything pleasant that he was summoned and instinctively he grew wary and suspicious. His mood was not dispelled by Scholes' manner.

For some moments after he had knocked and entered the chief continued writing. As Edgley stood waiting his resentment grew. Then glancing up casually Scholes remarked: "I was hoping to have those costs before this, Edgley. What's holding them up?"

PART 1: THE BITERS BITE

The fact was that Edgley was behind because he had not been given the job in time, the delay being wholly the fault of Scholes. Moreover since getting the figures Edgley had worked hard and continuously. The unjustified attack therefore made him see red. All the same he controlled himself and replied courteously enough: "Holding them up? Nothing, sir. They ought to be finished tomorrow. There's a lot of work in them and I think I've got on fairly well."

"Oh you do, do you?" Scholes returned nastily. "Well, output like that may be good enough for you, but it's not good enough for the firm. Those costs should have gone to the manager tonight, and what am I to tell him tomorrow? If I plead incompetent staff he'll say, 'Change them!' "

It was this remark which tipped over the balance of Edgley's self-control. Something broke in his mind and the accumulated resentments of months poured out.

As he walked slowly towards his uninviting "bed-sit" and the unappetizing meal which was his landlady's idea of supper, he forced eyes and feet away from the bars he passed. He wanted something to ease the tension of his mind and substitute a feeling of happy content. But resolutely he told himself that he had made a fool of himself sufficiently for one evening. To get drunk might be pleasant for the moment, but it would not alter the circumstances, merely leaving him with less money to meet them.

When later in the evening he settled down to take stock of his position, he found it not so bad as he had feared. He had still quite a bit of his gratuity money, and this would keep him for at least some weeks while he was looking round. Jobs in plenty he could of course get if he were not particular as to their nature. But not of the kind he wanted. In all he would be in a wholly subordinate position, a position of soul-destroying impotence, at the mercy of ignorant clerks or foremen or union bosses. He had had enough of that in the office he had just left.

Before joining up Edgley had been employed in a bank and because he could speak French he had been sent to the Paris branch. But on demobilization he had felt too restless for bank routine and had turned down the offer of his old job. He had tried for many positions which offered at least a partially out-of-doors life together with the exercise of judgment and initiative, only to find that these were reserved for the favoured few who already had a record of success in just such undertakings. In the end he had taken the job with the builder, hoping sometimes to get out on the works. In this he had been disappointed.

What he really wanted was to have lived fifty or a hundred years earlier when there were still uncharted lands to conquer. A settler in a new country! That was what he would have liked. To be on his own, up against nature. To have the job of creative work. To break in virgin land. To marry some like-minded girl who would come out with him and rough it, so that together they could force a livelihood from reluctant surroundings. That was a man's life! But none such seemed to offer today.

The possibility which he most seriously considered was entry into the police. It was a good service and one for which his commando training would be useful. The chief snag was that once again he would have to begin at the bottom of the ladder, but no doubt time would overcome this difficulty.

In all probability he would have applied to some constabulary for a start, had not something happened to turn his thoughts in an entirely fresh direction. One day as he was rounding the corner from Regent Street into Piccadilly he met Loxton.

PART 1: THE BITERS BITE

Dick Loxton was a lifelong friend. They had been playmates since they could toddle, their parents living near one another on the outskirts of Poole. Loxton had early become the proud possessor of a boat, and the boys had spent more of their time on the water than ashore. They had gone to the same school, and when Edgley had started in the bank, Loxton had entered the office of a well-known publisher, not quarter of a mile away. Both had volunteered for service when war broke out, but while Edgley went into the army, Loxton chose the navy. During the war they had drifted apart and since its conclusion neither had known the other's whereabouts. The meeting was therefore all the greater surprise and pleasure.

"Jove, Peter, it does one good to see you again," Loxton declared after their first greetings. "How're things? Come and have a drink and let's hear the news."

Over pints of mild and bitter they exchanged experiences. Loxton had been held in the navy and was not long back in civvy street. He was somewhat vague as to his movements. He had not decided what to go in for and was looking round. The only thing he was sure of was that he had finished with publishing.

"How's that, Dick?" Edgley asked. "I should have thought it a good job. Interesting too."

"It may be, but not to me," Loxton answered. "I tell you, Peter, I just can't face that sort of thing any more. I don't know how it is, but the war has unsettled me. I want to be doing things out of doors, not poring all day over papers in my office."

Edgley nodded. "Just my trouble. I've tried it in a builder's office. Couldn't stick it. Miserable pettifogging little jobs. Niggling for days over things that could be fixed up in five minutes. And no prospects. Ghastly!"

ANYTHING TO DECLARE?

"Then what are you doing now?"

"Nothing. Should say, wondering what I'm going to do." Loxton hesitated. "Anything in view?" he said, with an assumption of carelessness which suddenly interested Edgley.

"Not a thing," he answered. "Been considering the police, but I'm not keen on it."

"No, I shouldn't be either. What did you do in the war? Let's have a bit of autobiography."

Edgley gave an abbreviated synopsis. Loxton seemed interested. For a moment he looked at his friend in an appraising questioning way. Then without speaking he took their glasses for two more pints. As he sat down again he raised his own. "To jobs for both of us that we like!" he toasted.

"Drink to that all right," Edgley agreed. "But I don't see much chance of it, not for me at least."

Loxton was silent for a moment, then bent forward more confidentially. "Talking of another matter, Peter, I'd like to know your ideas about breaking the law."

Edgley stared, then laughed. "Bit unexpected, that. What's behind it? Do I look that much of a rogue?"

"No," Loxton said seriously, "you look honest, which is a considerable asset if you want to try the other. I'm not joking, Peter. I really want to know your views."

Edgley's interest curve rose sharply. "Got something up your sleeve?" he insisted.

"Perhaps I have, but I want a serious answer to my question."

"Rum question and no mistake. I've no objection to breaking the law as such. All depends on what's to be done. I'm not specially on for murder or treason or stealing a blind man's coppers. Otherwise I don't care two hoots."

PART 1: THE BITERS BITE

"Any objection to a legal fraud, provided no individual person is hurt?"

"Not me. Matter of fact it sounds attractive. What is it? Don't tell me you've no proposition."

"No, I won't tell you that. But I don't think this is a good place to discuss it. For me the open spaces. What about a seat in Hyde Park?"

"Far from the madding crowd?"

"You've said it."

They walked along Piccadilly, chatting of their war experiences, and eventually found a couple of chairs standing alone.

"I have an idea at the back of my mind," Loxton resumed when they were seated, "and I wonder if you'd be interested? As a matter of fact it's not my own, it was put up to me by a man named Baldwin. He acted as paymaster on my ship and I got to know him rather well. A good sort and pretty able too."

"Navy man?"

"Only for the duration. But a point before I go on. I know it's not necessary with you, Peter, but I must say it formally. All this is in the strictest confidence. That all right?"

"Hang it all, Dick! What do you take me for? Course it's all right."

"I knew that. Then about this chap Baldwin. He owns a microscopic manufacturing plant in Canterbury. I've been over it. Well run and all that, but I should say too small really to pay. In fact, that's the actual situation. We talked it over and he admitted it himself."

"A good opening, Dick. Why'd you not stick to publishing?"

"Well, there's more to come. But first I must tell you a bit more about myself. Under the pater's will I have a small income. It's only a hundred a year, nothing like enough to live on, but useful as far as it goes."

"Should think so indeed."

"Then my Uncle Sydney died. You remember him perhaps?"

"Of course. Great yachtsman."

"That's the chap. Well, he left me an unexpected legacy: a motor cruiser. She's a fine boat. She's 75 feet long and weighs 46 tons, with a Leyland Diesel main engine and a Gray for stand-by and slow running. A normal top speed of 10 knots, but she'll push up to 12 if necessary."

"My word, Dick, some boat and no mistake. What are you going to do with her?"

"Well, that's it. I'll show you her plan if you'll come round to where I'm staying, but I may tell you now that besides my own and the crew's quarters she has two quite decent two-berth cabins, a dining saloon, a deck saloon with a settee berth, and quite a good deck space, including a forward sun deck."

"Damn it, Dick, you sound like a cruise advertisement."

"Well, that's pretty much what it is. Let me finish. She has Calor gas fires in saloons and cabins and hot and cold water in cabins and bath. Wireless in the deck saloon, large galley and store: in fact, about everything you could want for a longish cruise. And the fittings and finish are quite first class."

"Name, the *Paragon*? Go on, what are you going to do with her?"

"First I thought I'd have to sell her: I couldn't afford to keep her. Then I heard of a chap with a somewhat similar boat who was doing cruises. He had several alternatives. In the summer he went from London to the South Coast, or up the Seine to Paris, or through the waterways of Belgium

PART 1: THE BITERS BITE

and Holland, and so on. The idea is that people make up their own party of four or five and charter the yacht from a Saturday to a Saturday for one, two, three or four weeks. This chap, the owner, runs the ship and he has a one-man crew and a chef-steward. He takes the party wherever they want to go."

"It's an idea."

"A snag to most people is the cost. He charges something like thirty pounds a week per head."

Edgley considered this. "Sounds a lot. But hang it, not so much when you consider what you're getting for it."

"You think not?"

"Course I think not. Look at what you pay in any decent hotel. The balance for the travelling seems reasonable."

"Maybe you're right. Well, what occurred to me, or rather to my friend Baldwin, was that as this chap can only take five at a time, there might, out of a population of some fifty millions, be another five anxious to go."

"Sure to be, I'd say."

"So I thought I'd try the same game. You think the idea okay?"

Edgley changed his position. "It would take quite a bit of money to finance the thing before you got returns. That be all right?"

"I couldn't afford a penny."

Edgley grinned. "Then you've more in your mind than you've mentioned. Come on, over with it."

"As a matter of fact it's Baldwin. For a partnership Baldwin would finance the start."

"That's certainly different. Tell me, Dick, are you serious about this?"

"Absolutely."

"Oh. Got your crew?"

"I'm beginning to hope so. What would you think of Peter Edgley?"

Edgley sat up with a jerk. "Me?" he exclaimed. "You mean that, Dick?"

"Would you consider it?"

"Consider it? I'd leap at it blindfold! But you could do a lot better than me, you know, old chap. Fond enough of boats and all that, but I'm only an amateur."

"You'd suit the job, but the job mightn't suit you. It's not so simple as it sounds. I'd want to run the thing with just the two of us. That would mean pretty hard work for you. I'd be in charge on deck all the time, steering and so on, and you'd have to do all the rest. Engineer, greaser, deck hand and crew generally you'd manage all right, but how about the other side of it?"

"Meaning?"

"Meaning cabin steward, chef, caterer, and general servant to the passengers."

Edgley's heart sank. "Oh," he grunted. "I'm no cook, you know, Dick."

"If that's the only trouble, you could learn. Some alterations would be required on the yacht and we couldn't start for several months. You could mug up a bit of theoretical knowledge from books and then get a job in some hotel for the practical side. How does that strike you?"

"I'd do it if I could. Like a shot. No hesitation at all."

"But what about cleaning the ship and cabins, making beds, taking orders from the passengers and all that?"

"Oh," Edgley demurred, "not so nice. But there's a snag in everything. Doesn't matter, I'm on just the same. Tell you, Dick I'd rather do it than anything else I can think of."

PART 1: THE BITERS BITE

"My idea would be to run not more than eight hours a day or perhaps ten at a pinch. We'd tie up at night and possibly during the midday meal. I mean, I'd rather want a spot of sleep sometimes and maybe something to eat as well. You'd have to relieve me at the helm occasionally, and when we're at anchor I'd help you with your job."

"Okay. Working like that I could do it."

"Then I'd propose a different tour to that other chip. I'd concentrate on the Rhine. The Rhine's a great river and there's a lot to see along it. Start from Margate or Ramsgate, cross to the other side and follow the coast up to one of the mouths. Then up the river as far as Basle, spending a fortnight on the trip."

"I've been on a bit of it, between Cologne and Mainz. A good trip."

"I've not worked out details yet, but I thought we'd go straight through to Cologne, except for a stop at Arnhem for a look at the battlefields. Then between Cologne and Mainz there'd be some five days for excursions: Wiesbaden, Bad Ems, Heidelberg and so on. Back to sleep on the yacht at night, you understand. From Mainz to Basle I imagine there's less to see, but we'd go into all that later."

"Why go above Mainz?"

"The idea would be that after a fortnight in the yacht our passengers would want a change. They'd have three days in Switzerland. That wouldn't be part of the trip: they'd go on their own where they liked. Then we'd come back down the river in the same way, but a little quicker and with different excursions. I reckon we could do from Basle home in ten days."

"Easily, I should think. That's four weeks altogether?"

"Five really, because at the end of each trip there'd be a week for cleaning and refitting and minor repairs. I'd propose to run from the beginning of April to the end of September. That would give us five trips in the season."

"And in the winter?"

"Lay up. No good trying to run after October."

Edgley did not reply. The first keen edge of his delight in the proposal had become somewhat blunted. This was by no means a sure money-maker. On the other hand Loxton was no fool and there must be more in the scheme than he had explained. Edgley decided to attempt some probing. "Some snags, I'm afraid, old man," he began tentatively.

"I know there are. What do you make them?"

"Suppose you don't get your passengers for some trips. What then? The yacht'll eat money and so will the crew. So even will the captain."

"And you think we wouldn't make it out of other trips?"

"Well, would we? Come on, Dick, what's the whole story? All that about breaking the law? That must come in somewhere."

Loxton made a sudden gesture. "You're right of course, Peter. There's more in it than I've told you. We propose to make our money by breaking the law. That's why I asked you those questions. Are you still on?"

Edgley chuckled. "If it's anything very bad like abducting children or handing over our most cherished secrets to the Russians, I reserve the right to contract out."

Loxton smiled in his turn. "If it'll ease your mind, it's not political. But joking apart, it's not a popular proceeding with the government. If we're caught we'll go to prison. That make you think?"

"Much chance of being caught?"

"Very, very little at first and for a long time to come, probably several years. In the unlimited long run I should

PART 1: THE BITERS BITE

say discovery was a dead cert. Therefore we propose to run for a time and then quit."

"Then prison hinges on your judgment of the time to get out?"

"That would be true if you substituted our collective judgment for mine."

"Fair enough. Okay, I'm on. What's the big idea?"

Loxton looked regretful. "I'm sorry, Peter, but before I can tell you Baldwin will have to agree. You see, the idea's his and he's putting up the cash, and if there's a hitch he'll go to prison too. You must meet him first, but as the police say when they ask you where you were at the time of the murder, it's only a matter of form."

"Where's the great man to be found?"

"At Canterbury, but neither you nor I can go there. Under no circumstances must our connection with him become known."

"Sounds good. Then how do I meet him?"

"He'll drive round, pick us up separately and talk in the car, then set us down in the same way."

Edgley grinned. "Fine! I'm going to like this."

"It's not going to be all beer and skittles I can tell you. We're going to work for our money." Loxton glanced at his watch. "Just getting on to seven. Baldwin should be home by now. I see a call-box on the road over there. I'll ring him up, then what about a spot of dinner?"

Edgley was in a very different mood from that of a couple of hours earlier. Hope, interest, even excitement seethed in his mind. Here at last was the chance he had been longing for! Action, constant change of scene, the pitting of himself against difficulties! And under what conditions: touring the Rhine in a yacht with the companionship of that splendid chap Loxton! What more could anyone desire?

If the illegal element was a drawback, and of course it was, it would at least supply the one element needed to make the prospect perfect: excitement. Morally it couldn't be very bad. Loxton was a decent fellow, and wouldn't lend himself to anything really shady.

Presently the man returned. "Baldwin's engaged tomorrow, but next day he'll meet us. I'm to join him near Rochester and we'll drive towards Maidstone. You leave the centre of Maidstone at ten and walk towards Rochester. We'll pick you up about half past."

For Edgley time dragged during the next day. On the following morning he set off early, eager for what might be coming. He reached Maidstone before his time and strolled for half an hour about the pleasant little town. Then he tramped off along the Rochester road.

It was just on to half past ten when a light green car came in sight, drew in to the kerb and stopped beside him. Loxton leaned out. "Jump in, Peter." Edgley did so and the car moved off.

In the driving seat was a middle aged rather ruthless looking man with a square jaw, thin compressed lips and sharp intelligent eyes. Loxton turned to him.

"This is Peter Edgley, Baldwin. Bruce Baldwin, Peter." They asked each other how they did and were thus officially friends.

"Baldwin's been decent about this, Peter," Loxton went on. "Though you're a stranger to him he doesn't want any information about you. I've told him you'd be a help to us and he's letting it go at that."

"If Dick Loxton's satisfied about anyone, that's good enough for me," Baldwin declared. "Glad to welcome you into this company of thieves. I hope we'll have some profitable times."

PART 1: THE BITERS BITE

"Well," Edgley answered, "you're both making it easy for me. Glad to join in and try to pull my weight. Same time, as I understand we may be run in at any moment, I'd be glad to know what the charge is likely to be."

Baldwin smiled a little grimly. "Of course you would, though I hope arrest is not so imminent as you suggest. But first let's find a quiet place and pull up."

He had turned off the main road and they were now passing along a deserted lane beneath trees. Presently topping a low hill they came to open ground with before them a fine extended view of the weald. Baldwin drew on to the grass at the side.

"Stopped to admire the prospect," he declared. "Very natural to pull up here." He switched off the engine. "Now, Loxton, you're better at talking than I am. Start in and tell our friend what we propose."

"Okay," said Loxton. "But what about a small preliminary?" He turned to Edgley. "Open that case beside you, Peter, and you may find something helpful. Any ideas, Baldwin?"

"No spirits for me. Beer if there is any."

The case was well equipped and three glasses of beer were soon in service. While they were drinking they chatted idly, but when bottles and glasses were back in the case Loxton turned to business.

"I didn't explain, Peter, the nature of Baldwin's plant in Canterbury, but the moment I do so you'll guess what's in our minds. He makes watches."

Edgley wondered if he was being stupid, but he did not at once see light. "Yes?" he said doubtfully.

"Perhaps I shouldn't say it in Baldwin's presence," went on Loxton, grinning at his friend, "but the organization of the place is good: real American scientific management. You make few types of watches, but a lot of each type: isn't that right?"

"Yes, the tools for the parts are costly and we don't reset them more often than is necessary."

"In spite of that the business is not paying. How do you explain that, Baldwin?"

"Well, you're not quite correct there, Loxton. The business pays, but only about enough to keep going. It's too small and I haven't the cash to enlarge. I've considered closing down, but all my savings are in the plant and without it I'd have nothing at all to live on."

"And you've thought of a way to increase the profits?"

"The point of our meeting," Baldwin declared. "Your turn again, Loxton."

"It's a simple notion, but we think profitable. Baldwin proposes to add to his business an agency for the sale of Swiss watches."

"That's it," Baldwin agreed. "There's a tremendous market for them in this country. Of course they're expensive owing to the duty."

A light shone belatedly in Edgley's mind. "You mean to smuggle them in and sell them cheap?" he exclaimed.

"Not quite," Loxton answered. "We mean to smuggle them in, but not to sell them cheap."

"I think I see. Make it pay by saving the duty?"

"That's the idea. Every trip of the launch will bring in some hundreds of watches. As I told you, we propose to get rid of our passengers at Basle, go on up the river for a few miles and load the watches at night. Then we have a week at home between trips. We'll lie up in the Stour and run the watches to Baldwin's works, also at night."

For the second time since he had met Loxton a feeling of disappointment overcame Edgley. This sounded all right as

PART 1: THE BITERS BITE

an idea, but it wouldn't be so easy in practice. A flood of watches on the market would inevitably become known and all possible entrance channels would be suspect, the yacht among the others. Customs officers weren't fools. If suspicion were once aroused they'd find the watches, even if they took the yacht apart rivet by rivet. Still, as he thought before, Loxton was scarcely the man to back a dud scheme. It was a case for suspended judgment.

"It sounds good if you could do it," he answered. "But I fancy there'd be snags."

"There certainly are. What snags do you see?"

"I take it," Edgley questioned, "you'd sell what you had wholesale to watchmakers and jewellers? You wouldn't attempt any retail trade direct to the public?"

"That's right."

"Well, surely if a firm was found selling watches, they'd be asked where they got them, so as to check up that the duty was paid? They'd give Baldwin's name, and there you'd be."

The others smiled. "That was an early headache," Loxton returned, "but we think we've got over it. In the first place it's by no means certain that any questions would be asked. Large numbers of shops do sell Swiss watches, all brought in quite legally. Therefore there's nothing in such sales to arouse suspicion."

"That may be," admitted Edgley. "Same time I shouldn't care to trust my freedom from prison to it."

"He's right," put in Baldwin. "As a matter of fact neither would we. Explain it to him, Loxton."

"To meet the difficulty Baldwin proposes to start up a legitimate trade at the same time. He's found a chap, a man who served with him in the navy, who'll take on the job of Swiss agent to buy the watches. Speaks perfect French and

German. He'll send them to Baldwin by legitimate routes. Duty will be paid and the transaction will be wholly correct. But he'll not send all he buys that way. For every watch that comes in legitimately, two will travel duty free by the yacht."

Edgley hesitated. "Sounds all right," he said doubtfully.

Loxton laughed. "I admire your enthusiasm. But just think it out. Baldwin sells smuggled watches to Firm X. Some government Johnnie smells a rat and asks the X people where they got them. They say, 'From Baldwin'. The Johnnie goes to Baldwin and says, 'How did you get those watches into the country?' Baldwin says, 'By post' or 'As overland freight' as the case may be, and turns up Customs receipts. Obviously the receipts won't be for those particular watches, but for others of the same type which came in legitimately. But the Johnnie won't know that. And there's no way in which he could find out, no matter how suspicious he was."

Again Edgley hesitated. "May be right enough," he said at last, "but surely if the Customs were suspicious they'd find that Baldwin sold more watches than were covered by the receipts?"

"How could they? Baldwin would be careful never to sell to any *one* firm more than he had receipts for. Same way he would never sell any type of watch for which he hadn't Customs receipts."

"In practice," put in Baldwin, "I wouldn't sell to any *three* firms more than I had receipts for. The Customs people would never hit on more than three firms I'd supplied."

Edgley grinned. "You seem to have covered it all right."

"I should have said that the watches will come in without wristbands. Baldwin will make and put these on."

"Why that? Should be Swiss too, shouldn't they?"

PART 1: THE BITERS BITE

"It's to save space on the yacht really. As you can imagine, the space for watches is strictly limited. No good in using it for straps, which can be supplied as well in England."

"I've got that. Is it a fair question to ask where you carry the watches on the yacht?"

"Well, it's a bit complicated and you'd follow more easily if you saw it. We'll show it to you, but meantime take our word that we can do it."

Baldwin laughed suddenly. "Tell the poor beggar what he's panting to know, Loxton: how much he is going to get out of it."

Edgley smiled in his turn. "Well, yes, Baldwin's right. I was going to ask you really."

"It's the kernel of the whole thing, isn't it?" Loxton agreed. "I can tell you, but only approximately. We propose to carry 2,000 watches on each trip. With five trips that's 10,000 in the season. We think for safety's sake we should confine ourselves to a cheap class of watch, which is common over here. On each watch we reckon the duty would be from one to two pounds, say, a profit of £15,000 a year."

Edgley stared. "Good Lord!" he gasped.

"Ah, but it's not so healthy as it looks," Loxton went on. "We're counting that at least £2,000 may be needed to help the running of the yacht, if we don't get a paying load of passengers. Then we'll have to pay Baldwin's advance for altering the yacht and various other expenses: say another thousand. That would leave us about £12,000 to be divided among us."

"Twelve thousand!" Edgley repeated in an awestruck voice as if overwhelmed.

"It's still not as good as it looks. First there'll be six of us in it: we don't think we could run the scheme with less. Then each of us will get proportionately to what we put in. You put in your work. I put in my work and the yacht as well, so I'd get more than you. But I'd say you'd be safe for £1,500 a year. That right, Baldwin?"

yes, at least that. The idea is that the six of us would agree what percentage of the profits we'd each get, and then we'd get that percentage. Matter of simple arithmetic."

"I'd do a lot for £1,500 a year," Edgley declared earnestly.

Baldwin grinned at him. "You mean you want to carry on with us?"

"You bet I do."

"Then you should avoid me like poison, and if we chance to meet, remember we're not acquainted. Well, that about finishes us for now. I'll put you down when we get to the main road and you fix up with Loxton what you're to do."

Ten minutes later Edgley was on his way back to London, his head swimming with all he had to think about.

– 2 –

THE PREPARATIONS

Beyond telling him that he should get a book on plain cooking and begin to mug it up, Loxton had given Edgley no directions as to his preparation for the part of "crew" on the yacht. It was not indeed until the third day that Edgley heard from him again. Then a telegram suggested lunch at a West End restaurant.

"There's no reason why we shouldn't be seen together," Loxton said when they had found an isolated table. "It will soon become known that we're jointly running the yacht, and therefore it's natural enough that we should foregather ashore. All we've to keep secret is our connection with Baldwin."

"Follow that all right. What about the other three chaps in the thing?"

"You'll meet them shortly. Meanwhile what have you been doing?"

"Roasting, boiling, cutting chickens, making pastry – in my dreams. Nightmares rather. Fed up with the job already."

"Good," Loxton returned. "Well, I've got your practical training fixed up. And jolly lucky you are. My cousin's taking you on – for a consideration."

"Your cousin?"

ANYTHING TO DECLARE?

"Betty Bramwell. She's manageress and part-owner of a private hotel near Surbiton. She's interested in the venture. Shouldn't be surprised if she made up a party and came with us some time."

"Am I supposed to go there every day?"

"Yes. You start in the kitchen, and after that she coaches you in catering, table waiting, bedroom stewarding: every mortal thing you want to know."

"Does she, by Jove? Just my line if she's young and easy to look at."

"It's your line if she was the witch of Endor. No playing around with Betty, my son. This is a serious job of work."

"You're telling me. But seriously, Dick, I'm not too happy about the thing. I don't want to let you down."

"Don't be an ass, of course you won't. It's not as if we had to start tomorrow. You've months to get it up."

"It'll take them."

Loxton made a gesture of impatience. "Oh, have sense for a change. Look here, Peter, there's something else I want to ask you. What about cash? Here's October. We don't start till March and we probably don't get our first rake off till May or June. Can you carry on?"

Edgley thought this over. "Don't know that I can, Dick," he said at last. "I can manage for about four months, perhaps five. But that would be about my limit."

"Then you'd better have an advance. Besides you'll have expenses. You can't expect Betty to pay for the food you ruin. Also she must get something against the gas and electricity you waste. Then you'll want uniforms and so on."

"Uniforms?"

"Yes, yachting blue or white. A white linen coat. I'll dress up as skipper. Make the thing look better."

PART 1: THE BITERS BITE

"Okay, if you feel that way. Afraid in that case I should want something."

"Right. It'll be from Baldwin, you understand: a loan to be deducted from our first payment. Would a hundred do?"

"Too much."

"Not a bit of it. Now one other question and I'm through. When we were kids you were something of a carpenter. Kept it up?"

Edgley looked interested. "Well, yes, I have rather. Took a course at school and when I was at the bank I had a small workshop. When the parents were alive, you know, and before I went to Paris. Made a few bits of furniture for the house: hard woods with careful finishing: cabinet-making really. On the whole they weren't too bad."

Loxton glanced round. They were early and the restaurant was not yet full, but instinctively he leant forward and lowered his voice. "Could you alter some of the wooden fittings of the yacht without giving away that an amateur had been at work?"

Edgley whistled soundlessly. "Have a heart, Dick! How could I tell? Depends on the job. What have you in mind?"

"Rather tricky work, I'm afraid. I could scarcely explain, but we'll go down and have a look at it tomorrow."

"Where's the yacht lying?"

"Littlehampton. Up the river."

"You leaving her there all the winter?"

"Have to. At present I've no place else to put her. But she'll be all right. Moored fore and aft and afloat even at low springs."

Edgley leant forward and there was a light in his eyes. "I tell you, Dick, I'm glad I met you. Can't think of anything I'd like more than doing a decent carpentry job. And so helpful for my cooking."

"You'll just have to make a better pull out when you start the cooking. Well, we needn't sit here for the entire afternoon. If you've finished we'll go."

An hour later they reached Surbiton and the Elmtree Hotel. Betty Bramwell was there and saw them at once. She did not quite attain to Edgley's ideal of youth and beauty, but she greeted them pleasantly, though her manner was a little sharp. Edgley was impressed by the comfort and general excellence of the hotel and realized that to run such a place successfully a manageress could not be too easy going. She seemed interested in the yacht venture. "After all I'm doing for you, you'll have to take me for half nothing," she declared when they had fully discussed Edgley's tuition. It was presently decided that he should start work in three weeks' time, when the alterations to the launch should be complete. He was formally introduced to the chef, who when he found Edgley could speak to him in the scurrilous argot of the Paris slums, greeted him like a brother.

Next morning the two friends met at Victoria and took an early train for Littlehampton. It was bright and sunny in the little town with a pleasant breeze coming in from the sea. Loxton led the way to a small establishment on the river bank which displayed a board bearing the legend: "Silas Judd & Son. Boatbuilders."

"Mr Judd about?" called Loxton, and a stout elderly man in a carpenter's apron approached.

"Morning, Mr Judd," went on Loxton. "Nice day. This is my friend, Mr Edgley."

"Morning, sir. Morning, Mr Edgley. Want to go aboard?"

"Yes, please. How's trade?"

"Not too bad, sir. In fact surprisingly good. They say there's no money in the country, but I've got all the orders I can handle: mostly small racing yachts."

PART 1: THE BITERS BITE

"You're lucky."

"It's a fact: I admit it. But there's a snag in everything. I've got the orders, but I can't get the men. Not men like the old craftsmen who took a pride in doing a job well."

"I seem to have heard something like that before. Well, Mr Judd, nothing about the *Komforta*?"

"No, sir, she's all right. I went over her Saturday and she's in good shape."

"Fine. Thank you very much. Mr Edgley and I are coming to live for a week or two on board."

"Well, you could do worse. She's as comfortable a boat as I've seen."

"That's why I called her *Komforta*. It's an Esperanto word meaning comfortable."

"She's well named."

"I don't know if I told you I'm going to use her for tours next summer. Canals and rivers on the Continent. So if you care to put up a few hundreds for fares, we'll take you and your friends along."

"I wouldn't mind going and I wish you luck."

"Come aboard and drink to it. We want to make one or two small alterations, cupboards and so on, and we'll do it when we're aboard. I think we can manage ourselves, but if we get stuck we'll come to you for help."

"Glad to do anything, sir. But I'll not go aboard, if you don't mind. I want to get on with my job."

They had been walking towards the water, and as Judd spoke he brought out a couple of sculls from a store. Then he pulled in a small dinghy and held it while the others embarked.

"Thanks," said Loxton. "We'll probably be bothering you for odds and ends."

"Anything I can do."

Loxton pulled easily upstream. As they approached the *Komforta* Edgley grew more and more impressed by her size and lines.

"Why, she's not a launch," he exclaimed. "She's a ship; a small cruiser."

"Matter of fact she's officially a yacht," Loxton answered with satisfaction. "Not bad looking, is she? And she's better aboard."

She was flush decked throughout, except that in the very stern a couple of steps led down to a small area at a lower level. From this a clear promenade deck stretched forward to the wheelhouse amidships, which, save for a stumpy mast, was the highest structure aboard. Then in front of the wheelhouse came the deck saloon, and forward of it a raised sun deck some twelve feet by ten. Forward of this the deck curved in rapidly to the stem. On her starboard quarter a good-sized dinghy swung inboard on davits.

Over the rail of the low level deck astern hung a small companion ladder, and to this Loxton brought the dinghy. Edgley stepped aboard. He was amazed at the spaciousness of the deck and by the excellent fittings everywhere.

"My word, Dick!" he exclaimed, "you're in luck. She's a millionaire's baby."

"Come below."

Loxton unfastened a small companion hatch on the lower after deck and they went down. Aft of the steps and filling the entire stern was a good sized cabin containing two beds. Forward were the captain's cabin, a bathroom, a lavatory, and another full width double-bedded cabin with private lavatory. All the fittings were of the best, and there was a most happy suggestion of space, light and comfort.

"The two saloons are further forward," Loxton explained. "Normally you reach them via the deck, but

PART 1: THE BITERS BITE

there's a way through here for emergency use." He opened a narrow door in the double-bedded cabin and Edgley, passing through, found himself in the engine room. He was not an engineer, so could not appreciate the extraordinary beauty which Loxton claimed for the motors, but they seemed massive enough to drive a craft twice the size.

Forward of the engine room was the dining saloon, with ample room for six round the table. The galley and sink were small, and Edgley's heart sank slightly as he looked at them, but there was a good space for stores in the comparatively large forepeak, where also he would sleep. In the bows was another lavatory and the anchor chain locker.

"All beyond words," he declared. "Wouldn't have missed it for anything on earth."

"You haven't seen it all yet," Loxton returned. "There's another saloon, a deck saloon. Come up."

Steps led from the dining saloon to a small but admirably furnished lounge. Forward of this was the sun deck. Edgley could imagine nothing more delightful than an easy chair on this on a fine day while the yacht moved up some thrilling reach on the Rhine.

"Tell you what, Dick, apart from watches you've a little gold mine in this boat," he said. "No one who once sees her could resist her."

"The cash is the snag," answered Loxton. "It's going to cost the devil of a lot to run her and there won't be so many willing to pay it."

"Can anyone – with the currency restrictions?"

"We think so. All our stores and so on we'll buy here. We've really only to pay wayleaves and harbour dues abroad, besides of course a few excursions. We're hoping to get reductions on all these on the grounds that we're helping to re-establish the German tourist industry. Now let's get down to these alterations, because if you can't do them we'll have to think up something else."

Loxton led the way back to the dining saloon. "Now here we're at the hub of the affair: its very heart. If this doesn't work the whole thing's off. I mean, how we carry the watches."

Edgley grinned. "What I've been waiting for since I joined up."

"Very well, look at that ceiling. That ceiling forms the sun deck above."

"I rather gathered that."

"The deck consists of three-quarter inch sheeting, carried on those two by four deck beams spaced, as you can see, two feet centre to centre. That single sheeting is both deck and ceiling and, again as you can see, the beams divide the ceiling into panels, long narrow panels athwart the ship."

"Visible to the naked eye."

"Quite, and as is also visible, each panel is fitted with a moulded lincrusta panel piece, glued on the bottom of the planks: a bit of decoration that's going to help us."

"Go ahead."

"Very well, we're getting on. Now we're going to hide our watches in the thickness of that deck: as you might say, between deck and ceiling."

Edgley felt a sharp pang of disappointment. Whatever might be possible, this obviously was not. Why, the deck had no thickness to spare. Still once again Loxton was no fool.

"I don't get you," Edgley declared. "Explain a bit more."

Loxton nodded. "I expect you're thinking that there's not enough thickness for the purpose. But you'll build up the thickness. You'll take off the lincrusta and plant fore and aft strips on the ceiling between the deck beams, leaving a two-inch space between each."

"Yes?" doubtfully.

"These spaces will make slots two inches wide and half an inch deep – the depth of the strips. But the slots must run the whole length of the deck. They'll be interrupted every two feet by the deck beams, so you'll have to cut away pieces from the top of the beams, so that the slots will go through from end to end."

"I think I've got that. You mean, leave the top of the deck beams cut in a sort of castellated way?"

"That's it. Then to make a floor for the slots you'll fix to the bottoms of the strips a sheet of eighth-inch composition board, and below that replace the lincrusta."

"It would never be noticed! By heck, Dick, you're on to something all right! I'm clear enough as far as making the slots goes, but look here, won't the ceiling be a fixture?"

"Yes, of course."

"Then how will you get the watches in and out?"

"Ah, that was the problem for a long time. But I think I've solved it. Come up to the deck saloon."

They went up the short companion.

"Now," went on Loxton, "from this row of three windows we look out over the sun deck or dining saloon roof. It stretches forward from just beneath the sill of the windows."

"Right."

"Opposite its end and inside the cabin, and of course just under the sill of the windows, you notice this moulding?"

"Right."

"It was this moulding which really gave me my idea. You're going to make that moulding moveable."

"Oh, yes?"

"When the moulding is taken off you will continue the slots through the bulkhead into this cabin, so that you can get at them all from here. Putting the moulding back into place will hide the slots and seal their ends."

As Edgley thought over the proposal he grew more and more enthusiastic. "It's a scheme!" he exclaimed warmly. "Good for you, Dick! It'll work and nothing'll ever be suspected!"

"I don't think we'll escape suspicion, but I'm hoping that if we're searched nothing will be found."

"Safe as a house! I said it was a scheme! But wait a mo," Edgley's voice changed, "once again how will you get the watches in and out? Those slots will be something like twelve feet long and you'll only be able to get at them from the end."

"That's been met. The watches will pack into little tin boxes just the size to slide along the slots. They'll be made to hook on to one another. When you push one in or out, all the rest will follow like wagons in a train."

"I'll hand it to you, Dick. I see our fortune's made!"

"There's one other thing, but it's simple. You'll have to make some alterations, say, in the shelving or something in the galley or forepeak. Something that Judd can see and that'll account to him for the carpentry."

"Perfect! Absolutely perfect!"

Loxton grinned. "I'm all for optimism myself, but you're going a bit fast, you know, Peter. We haven't settled the fundamental question yet: can you do it?"

Edgley did not consider this. "Oh yes, I can do it," he said promptly. "Given the material and a bit of help from you, I can do it. Take a bit of thought of course to work out details, but I'll manage it."

PART 1: THE BITERS BITE

On this happy note Edgley began to measure up the materials required. His idea was to get everything planed and cut to an exact size, so that each piece would fit accurately and drop into place.

"A short excursion for tonight," said Loxton when everything had been noted. "A mile or so upstream. But we mustn't be seen."

They passed the evening chatting, then about eleven turned in, having darkened the yacht so that nothing but the riding lights were showing. Then about two they came quietly on deck. Loxton drew the dinghy alongside and they got in.

The night was dark but fine. There was no moon, but the stars were bright and they could see dimly about them. A gentle breeze blew from the south west, making just enough sound to cover their movements, but not enough to impede them.

"All I want is to show you a place on the river," Loxton explained as he sculled silently upstream. "I've been along both banks and it's the best there is. It's where we'll have to load up our materials. You'll run them down from town in my car, and I'll meet you with the dinghy and scull them on board."

"Must be done at night?"

"Of course it must be done at night. And silently and without lights. No one must know that that material has come aboard."

Presently Loxton turned in to the left bank. "See," he said, "I'll come ashore here opposite those trees. You'll recognize them from the land. Now just back there a lane runs up to the road. You come down that lane with the car as far as you can, then carry the stuff the rest of the way."

"Sounds okay."

ANYTHING TO DECLARE?

"I suggest that you go ashore now, find the lane, follow it to the road and have a look round, so that you'll know where you are when you're driving down."

To Edgley this seemed sound sense and he carried it out. The bank was stony and he got ashore without sinking in mud. He quickly found the lane and noted a place where he could turn the car. Then he walked back to the road and saw where the lane struck off. Returning, he had no trouble in finding the dinghy.

"Fine," he said, as they paddled back to the yacht. "If everything's as good as this, we'll do."

As later that morning they returned to London Loxton turned to another subject.

"About ordering that stuff. When you do it you mustn't be recognizable. Have you considered disguises?"

Edgley hadn't, but he gave the matter careful attention when Loxton pointed out that if suspicion arose and if the purchase of the strips could be brought home to them, they would be as good as convicted. "They'd at once be on to what we've done," he declared. Very ordinary and hackneyed steps were, he pronounced, not only sufficient, but best. It was agreed that Edgley should insert false heels into his shoes to increase his height, put a wash on his face to darken his clear complexion, insert rubber pads into his cheeks to change the shape of his face, wear glasses and the clothes of a foreman joiner, dirty his hands and nails, and speak in as Cockney a voice as he could. Both thought that few would penetrate such a transformation.

That afternoon Edgley went to the East End and bought what he needed for the disguise and next morning, suitably arrayed, he ordered the materials together with the necessary tools.

PART 1: THE BITERS BITE

Meanwhile Loxton returned to Littlehampton, having first handed over the keys both of his car and of the shed in which it was garaged.

Two days later Edgley again assumed his disguise. Having taken out the car, he collected the strips and composition board, returning with them to the shed. Much of the afternoon he spent in tying the stuff up in easily carried bundles. Then about eleven he set off for Littlehampton. He drove slowly and carefully, so as not to risk a police holdup.

His rendezvous with Loxton was at one-thirty, and just about that hour he came to the lane, passed down it, and turned at the point he had decided on. Then switching off his lights, he picked up the first of his bundles and staggered off to the water's edge.

Loxton was waiting with the dinghy. He came ashore and helped Edgley with the remaining bundles, then set off for the yacht. Edgley, starting up the car again, left the lane unseen and returned to London.

Next day Edgley went back by train to Littlehampton and openly called on Judd to put him aboard. Immediately he set to work. First, with great care he peeled off the lincrusta from the ceiling, then began on the heavy job of cutting twenty-nine slots through the tops of each of the six deck beams. This took a week. Next came the screwing on of the strips, another slow job owing to the care needed to keep them exactly the right distance apart. The fixing up of the composition board and the regluing of the lincrusta followed. When at the end of a second week these were in place, the ceiling looked as if it had never been touched. Both men were satisfied that there was absolutely nothing to suggest what had been done.

There still remained the alteration to the moulding and to this Edgley now gave his attention. It was another difficult job, and he carried out many experiments before finally deciding on his plan. This was to mount the moulding along the bottom on hidden hinges. When pulled forward at the top it uncovered the ends of the slots: when pushed back it was held in place by pins dropped in through holes at each end. Here also no trace of the work showed. Alterations were next made to the galley shelving, so that if Judd came aboard he would see the work which had been done.

"Well, Peter," said Loxton on the day on which all was complete, "I'll certainly hand it to you. A cabinetmaker could have done no better job. And no living soul in the world except our two selves knows anything about it."

Edgley grinned. "Nothing in it," he protested. "Save your enthusiasm for my first meal. If the passengers survive I'll deserve everything you say."

"Don't worry: the human frame will stand a lot. Now let's see. Here's the end of October and we won't start running till early spring. You'll not be wanted till about mid-March, so that gives you nearly five months. If you can't cook and wait and steward and valet by the end of that time you may go out and commit suicide."

"Five months' practice? It should be a help."

"Baldwin's dealing with the watches and he'll get the tin holders made. My headache is permits, wayleaves, harbour dues, excursions and all that, and I propose to spend a few weeks on the Rhine learning my way about."

"I envy you that."

"I might be glad of your help. We'll see later. Then the other men have to get going, Harry Furnell, who'll collect the watches in Switzerland, and Valentine Dolbey, who'll

PART 1: THE BITERS BITE

take them ashore over here and run them to Baldwin's works at Canterbury."

"Fine. Thought there were six in it?"

"There's Edwin Campion, Baldwin's storekeeper. He's the sixth."

"My word, Dick, I'm looking forward to the thing! Cooking or no cooking, I wouldn't have missed it for all the world!"

"We've done all right so far. We should be ready for March."

Next day Edgley returned to Surbiton. Then began a strenuous and rather distasteful period of work at the hotel. He put up with it because he felt that gradually he was mastering his new job, but it was with unconcealed satisfaction that at last, towards the middle of March, he heard from Loxton that he was wanted on the yacht.

– 3 –

THE FIRST TRIP

Edgley's instructions were to travel by rail to Ramsgate and there look out for Valentine Dolbey, who would be seated in a Ford Prefect at the station. When the train left London it was dull and cloudy, but as they went further east the sky cleared, and at Ramsgate the sun was shining. Edgley did not exactly believe in omens, but the bright freshness of the air as he left the station seemed to put a final stamp of approval on this splendid adventure on which he had embarked.

There was only one Ford Prefect parked on the approach road and Edgley spoke to the driver. He was a rather dissipated looking young man, dark and hatchet-faced and with an unpleasant sardonic expression. But he answered civilly enough. "Yes, I'm Dolbey and I suppose you're Edgley. I've come to meet you. Just push your stuff into the back and get in with me."

"Loxton told me you were in charge down here," went on Edgley as he obeyed, "but he didn't give me details. Haven't a notion what to expect. The *Komforta*'s not far off, I presume?"

"She's in the Stour, lying at my place, or what's my place while the job lasts. The Syndicate has rented me a little cottage on the bank and I've got the right to moor craft opposite it."

PART 1: THE BITERS BITE

"Loxton said you were transport between the yacht and Canterbury?"

"Yes, that's right. But really we don't know each other's jobs. They thought that safer. For instance, I don't know what yours is, though I know you're to be on the yacht."

"No mystery about my job," Edgley grinned. "I'm cook."

Dolbey smiled. "That so? Well, they tell me an army marches on its stomach, so I suppose you'll be the kingpin of the entire outfit."

"Not only cook. General dishwasher and handyman and jack of all the trades no one else will touch. See me in my white jacket."

"You'll be meaning liaison officer with the public. You'll be glad to know that Loxton's got a full complement of passengers for the first trip."

"Good, that! Getting passengers seemed to me the snag in the whole affair."

"There's not much Loxton can't do."

They left the town westwards, circled Pegwell Bay, and drove south along the Stour. Then turning into a drive leading across one of the loops of the river, they reached a small square cottage set on the bank. Some amenities had been attempted. The tangle of tall marsh grass which covered the area had been cleared and a few windswept shrubs planted in its place. Ivy had been trained over the walls and the drive had recently been weeded. In spite of it the cottage looked somehow forbidding. Off it lay the *Komforta*.

"My humble abode," Dolbey explained rather unnecessarily. "If you'll be getting your stuff out I'll let Loxton know." He hoisted a red and blue flag on a small mast. "Sooner or later he'll see that and come ashore. In the meantime you'll have a drink?"

"Thanks, I'd like that," Edgley answered. "But look here," he pointed to a strange looking craft which was moored astern of the *Komforta*. "What on earth's that?"

Dolbey smiled and a sudden interest showed in his rather cold eyes. "Sure that's the explanation of my existence," he declared. "That's why I took my cottage and why I'm living here, and why I got permission to moor in the river."

"I can see that you had to explain your existence, but that craft's a new one on me. What is it, or is that not a tactful question?"

"Ah, not at all. It was put there for the very purpose that people might ask that question: *and* get a satisfactory answer. It's an experimental tide mill, a turbine driven by the tide. I've been working at the thing for years, and when this scheme came on sure didn't it seem a heaven-sent chance for a proper try out. So I made that a condition of joining. The others were only too pleased, for it was just the kind of cover they wanted."

"I'll say so. Lucky for both parties."

"If you're interested you must come aboard and see the great work. To be sure this is not the place I'd have chosen, for the tide here isn't strong enough. If the thing works the way I hope, I want to float a small company and try again at the entrance to Strangford Lough in Northern Ireland."

"Don't know it. Is there much of a run there?"

"Terrific. I'm told ten knots or more. If all goes well I propose to go over and see the place. I believe I could get enough electricity to run half Belfast."

"Pretty useful. Can I ask for details?"

"You can see the thing for yourself when we've had our drinks. Oh well, you can't now for there's Loxton. We'll go later."

PART 1: THE BITERS BITE

"Hullo, chef," presently came Loxton's voice. "Glad to see you, for I'm sick to tears of messing in that foul galley. Well, you've made friends with Dolbey?"

"Sure wasn't he just getting interested in my turbine when you barged in and spoiled it all. Have a drink?"

"A good thought. Lucky, Peter, that Dolbey wanted to play about with his toy. Couldn't have anything better to explain him to the natives. Well, tell me seriously how you've got on?"

"Seriously, Dick, I think not too badly. Believe I can produce a reasonable dinner. Was just telling Dolbey he should see me in my white coat."

"And a blue uniform?"

"Blue uniform also, tasteful and elegant."

"Catering?"

"Well, I can make a shot at that too. Did it for three weeks for the hotel, under supervision of course."

"Good for Betty. Well, that's important because you've got to stock up food for the party for four weeks. That's the nuisance of the currency restrictions: everything possible must be bought here. But we've got a fine, big fridge fitted in the forepeak."

"Be a help."

"You'll be pleased. We've built you off a little cabin, and the larder's a whole lot better. Come and see it. Thanks for the drink, Dolbey."

They went aboard and Edgley was shown the alterations. When he had fully admired them he turned the conversation to Dolbey. "Where did you come across him?" he asked.

"At sea. We met on different adventures. Good chap."

"Is he really keen on that tide affair or is it just part of the game?"

"Oh quite genuine. He's a trained engineer and he was working on it before this thing blew up. He's a nephew of Dr George Marsham, if you've heard of him."

"I haven't. That ignorance?"

"Well, I understand he's a pretty big pot in his own line. He was in Harley Street with quite a name until he got crippled with arthritis and had to give up."

"Couldn't heal himself."

"He's still supposed to be working on some theory that may revolutionize certain treatments: I don't know what. This Valentine Dolbey had a job with a firm of engineers in Folkestone and he happened to know of a vacant house in the suburbs. The old man liked it and took it and in return had Dolbey to live with him."

"If Dolbey was so well fixed, why did he leave?"

"Restless, I think."

"Well, if he's a good man and it's got us his help, I suppose we should be pleased. Tell me, did you do your trip along the Rhine?"

"Six weeks. I believe I now know the harbours and the worst sandbanks and so on."

"And the excursions?"

"And the excursions. I think we can offer a very good four weeks: a fortnight going up to Basle, three days in Switzerland and some ten days getting back."

"Any snags?"

"One rather unexpected one, bar the currency of course which is always a trouble. From here to Cologne is not so interesting: the best reaches are above that, between Cologne, and, say, Strasbourg."

"Rather imagined that myself."

"It's going to take five days to get from here to Cologne and another four from Cologne back. Now practically

PART 1: THE BITERS BITE

everyone I've talked to says: 'Why not take your passengers by air to Cologne and start the river trip there?' "

"Sounds reasonable. But of course we can't."

"That's just it. It's not only that the whole point of the trip is to bring the yacht from Switzerland to England, but it's necessary also because of the currency and catering."

"I see that."

"Naturally I've done what I could to make those nine days interesting. We have excursions to Amsterdam and Dordrecht; we have an afternoon in Nijmegen, and we call at Dusseldorf and Duisburg."

"Good enough, Dick. It's all fine. And there's the trip across the Straits. In good weather that'll please most people."

"That's so, and of course people like to step into a ship or coach or something they can stay in all the time: I mean no changing."

They chatted on for some time, then Loxton got down to business. Soon Edgley was preparing lists of stores. Loxton gave him a free hand. Edgley put down what he thought best, he bought where it seemed convenient, and he made his own arrangements – mostly with Dolbey's car – for getting the stuff on board. Loxton was also busy with stores; mostly nautical, but he disappeared from the yacht for days together, vouchsafing no explanation as to his whereabouts.

They made two or three short cruises on Pegwell Bay so that Edgley might learn enough of the ship to take over at any time from Loxton. Then at last the great day came.

That afternoon they left the Stour for Ramsgate, tying up at a convenient wharf about five-thirty. Half an hour later a lordly Rolls Royce appeared, from which descended two men and two women. These were Sir Malcolm and Lady Cairns and Mr and Mrs Lewis-Randall, well-known figures in London social life. Edgley learned later that they had been booked through the tourist agency of Joseph Butler & Son, and Loxton had taken them at an enormous reduction "to get the *Komforta* service known".

They were pleasant friendly people, as Edgley learnt almost from the first moment when he went out to conduct them on board and to see to their luggage. He had been concerned as to whether he should completely take the place of a steward, calling the passengers "sir" and "madam". Eventually he had decided not to do so, but to temper equality with extra politeness and a reasonable respect. With these people he found that this went down very well.

When they had been shown to their cabins there was a visit from the port authorities, after which Edgley cast off and Loxton took the yacht out to mid-harbour, there dropping anchor. The trip had been advertised as having no night travel, ostensibly to guarantee the passengers undisturbed rest, actually because the skipper and crew required some sleep themselves. Then came Edgley's first ordeal in the matter of dinner. He was pleased with the set-out of the table in the saloon. The spotless linen and gleaming silver and glass looked well against the yacht's dark panelling. Mellow reflecting ceiling lamps reinforced the light from the ports. The whole thing looked inviting and he overheard congratulations to Loxton on its appearance.

" 'Fraid I can't claim the credit, Sir Malcolm," Loxton answered grinning. "My friend Edgley is chef, purser, steward and crew generally. I hope you'll tell him if you're pleased, and I'm sure you will if you're not."

The dinner went well. The cooking was considered good, the meat tender and the coffee genuine. Everyone was

PART 1: THE BITERS BITE

pleased. When Edgley had washed up he joined the others in the saloon for a short time to establish his position. Then he and Loxton excused themselves on the plea of ship's business.

Next day was fine and by 8.00 a.m. they had left the harbour. There was a stiffish breeze, which had raised enough sea to make the yacht rather lively. To Edgley it was like old times, and once again he congratulated himself as he thought of the builder's office. The passengers appeared to be good sailors with the exception of Mrs Lewis-Randall, who at an early hour gracefully retired to her cabin. Skipper and crew were kept busy. Loxton could not leave the wheelhouse, and "housework" occupied every minute of Edgley's time. Rather to his surprise Edgley found that he was enjoying it. Already he was taking a pride in doing the work well, keeping the yacht spotless and supplying well cooked, well served and punctual meals.

That night they lay off Flushing and next day, following devious channels between the islands, they ran on to near the great Moerdijk bridges, which carry the main connections between Antwerp and Rotterdam. They arrived early enough to give the party a full afternoon in Dordrecht, for which Loxton had arranged a car.

"It's a success, Peter!" Loxton exclaimed when Edgley had returned from putting them ashore. "What do you think?" He spoke with unusual eagerness.

"Couldn't be better!" Edgley was frankly enthusiastic. "All as pleased as Punch! If we can carry on like this they'll give us a super ad and the thing may pay on the passengers alone."

"I don't expect that," Loxton returned. "But it'll be all to the good if we don't lose too badly over them."

ANYTHING TO DECLARE?

The run next day was not particularly interesting, owing to the flat country and the absence of important towns on the route. Just after tea they dropped anchor at Nijmegen, and here again Loxton had a car waiting to take the passengers to the battlefields. Dinner was put off till eight-thirty to give more time, and comments showed that the arrangements had been appreciated.

They were now meeting the full current of the river and their best speed was no more than about eight English miles per hour. It therefore took them till nearly five to reach their next port of call, Duisburg. Here Loxton had arranged no shore transport, leaving the passengers free to go where they liked.

From Duisburg to Cologne was a comparatively short run, and by two next afternoon they had reached the fine old city. Here the passengers had tea ashore, which pleased Edgley.

"Want to go ashore sometimes myself, you know," he explained somewhat mournfully to Loxton.

"Wait till the next trip," he was counselled. "You'll know better then what time you can spare." Edgley had to admit that the advice was good.

Next day they "did" one of the most spectacular reaches of the river, passing the Drachenfels and its six sister mountains on their way from Cologne to Coblenz. The weather was perfect and all four passengers spent their time lolling in chairs on the sun deck, obviously delighting in it. A four-hour call at Bonn in the middle of the day pleased them also.

The following day was welcomed by Edgley and Loxton, for they lay at Coblenz, while the tourists betook themselves ashore, visiting the town, as well as Bad Ems and the surrounding country. Though everything was going

PART 1: THE BITERS BITE

well, the trip was proving a strain. As both men had indeed foreseen, the work was really too much for them and they could have done well with a third hand. But when they turned their thoughts to the hoped-for reward, they were content to remain unaided.

Another day brought them to Mainz, with a four-hour halt at Bingen. Mainz meant two slack days for skipper and crew, as the party visited Frankfurt and Wiesbaden. Then on again, calling at Mannheim, Karlsruhe and opposite Strasbourg, in each case with a long afternoon ashore. Finally, a whole day's run took them from Strasbourg to Basle, where they arrived about six. Here the party transferred to an hotel in the town. The customs examinations at the various frontiers had given no trouble.

Earlier in the trip there had been some grumbling about having to leave the yacht at Basle. "Why can't we stay on board?" Mr Lewis-Randall had asked. "It seems a lot of unnecessary trouble to move to an hotel." Loxton, appealed to, had made a good case for it. "We have to clean the ship," he explained, "and take in stores. When we're taking in oil you wouldn't like it and," he grinned disarmingly, "you'd be in our way." That it was not only oil that they had to take aboard Loxton did not explain. As it turned out, when the time came the party seemed glad of a respite from the confined space aboard, and all passed off most amicably.

The passengers ashore, the yacht moved another few miles up the Rhine to the outskirts of a place named Kaiseraugst, anchoring off a small cottage just as she had done off Dolbey's house on the Stour. "That's Harry Furnell's," Loxton explained. "We don't know him except that we pay him for the privilege of anchoring off his ground. I'll go ashore for ten minutes tomorrow with the money."

"What about our cargo?"

"The dead of night for that. At 2.00 a.m. he's to bring the stuff across in his dinghy. We'll be waiting for him."

"Better a moonless night for the job."

"You're right. This is the one item in the entire affair I'm not too happy about. Seeing the river is the boundary between Switzerland and Germany there's a watch kept on it. We might get a searchlight on us at any moment. If that happened as the watches were being passed aboard it would take some explaining."

"My word, yes."

"I've been thinking of a plan to get over the difficulty, but it's not wholly satisfactory. To go ashore openly on arrival to pay our dues, and in returning to the yacht to bring with us the end of a line attached to the bank. Then in the night to pull backwards and forwards some small float which would sit too low in the water to be seen."

"What's wrong with that?"

"Well, we may want to discuss things with Furnell. It's convenient to have him aboard."

They were both tired after their fortnight's work, and from supper till it grew dark they sprawled lazily with pipes on the sun deck. Then Loxton got up. "I'm going to turn in," he declared, "and so should you. We want to be fresh at two."

Before lying down they carefully sealed all the portholes and windows, so that no light should escape from the deck saloon while they were loading the watches. In spite of his weariness Edgley could not sleep. As he understood it, they were now at the most critical stage of their enterprise. Discovery was not so impossible as he had expected from Loxton's previous statements, and discovery would be an unrelieved disaster. He did not know what would be the

PART 1: THE BITERS BITE

result. As they would not actually have done any smuggling, he did not see that they could be punished, but the enterprise would of course be killed dead. It was with eagerness that he lay awaiting zero hour.

Shortly before two they crept silently on deck and moved to the companion ladder hanging over the rail in the stern. The night was fine and clear with bright stars but no moon, and as Edgley's eyes grew accustomed to it, he found he could see further than he thought healthy. The yacht plucked gently at her anchor, swinging slightly from side to side in the current. There was no wind, but the flow of the river was audible, as well as the jabbling of little wavelets against the bows.

Though Edgley kept what he thought was a pretty sharp lookout, he saw nothing till there in front of him at the companion ladder a small dinghy suddenly loomed up. A dark crouching figure in it called softly: "Are you there, Loxton?"

"Okay, Furnell. Pass up the stuff."

The figure stooped and picked up a box some twelve inches square by six deep. It was of fair weight, but Loxton and Edgley caught it between them and laid it gently on the deck. Two other similar boxes followed and then Furnell climbed aboard.

"Let's get 'em to the saloon."

The three men, each carrying a box, crept softly along the deck and into the deck saloon. Then Loxton closed the door and turned on the light. "This is Edgley," he explained. "You've heard about each other, so I don't have to do any introducing. Well, Furnell, how have you got on?"

Furnell greeted Edgley, then turned back to Loxton. "Better than I could have hoped," he declared. "So far everything has gone like clockwork, or perhaps I should say, like watchwork."

"Tell us the story."

They sat down and poured out drinks. "Well," Furnell went on, "it's just that the scheme's going. I've got a fine connection with a number of watch-making firms. I've given fairly big orders and the stuff's coming in on time."

"All to your cottage?"

"No, no. Nothing comes here and no one knows I live here. I've taken a small place in Basle and it all goes there. I call it my collecting depot from which I send the stuff to England."

"Fine! That's better than Baldwin's idea. You can run that place openly."

"That's just it," Furnell nodded. "I do send from it a lot of stuff direct to Baldwin's works in Canterbury. It's all perfectly above board and I can produce the papers to prove it. It's a perfectly legitimate trade and any revenue people can come and inspect anything they like at any time."

"A bit of all right. Then the secret watches?"

"The secret watches come home in my car each evening, packed under food. I think it's quite safe."

"Sounds perfect. It means that if a certain watch is sold in England and the British revenue people question its origin, you can produce evidence that it went openly to Baldwin?"

"That's right. With the receipts for duty that Baldwin would be able to produce, the thing's absolutely watertight."

"Well, congrats and all that. Now what have you got for us?"

"The full quota: two thousand watches."

"You haven't? Oh fine, Furnell! That's magnificent! It means – let's see – about four hundred for you, Peter, on this one trip. What do you think of that?"

PART 1: THE BITERS BITE

Edgley felt overwhelmed. Five trips a year at four hundred pounds a trip! Two thousand a year! And the thing might run for six or eight or even ten years!

"I'm speechless!" he declared. "Couldn't have believed it! The most profitable bit of cooking I've ever taken on."

They chatted for a few minutes longer, then Loxton said they'd better get down to it. "Open up your moulding, Peter, and we'll shove the stuff in."

Edgley withdrew his two pins, then pulled the moulding forward on its hinges, revealing the ends of the slots hidden in the thickness of the deck. He was interested to see that all were filled with some kind of tin containers.

"Let's begin by getting out the empty holders," Loxton went on, pulling at one of the tins.

Edgley pulled at another and drew from the slot a box, some 12" long, 1½" wide and ⅜" deep. The top was hinged along one side and the whole exterior was covered with soft cloth. At each end was a hook, so contrived that it engaged with the hook of its neighbour. All ten holders in each slot were therefore coupled together like railway wagons, and when Edgley pulled, the whole ten came out one after another.

They soon had withdrawn the two hundred and fifty empty holders from the twenty-five slots. These made quite an imposing heap on the saloon floor. Then Furnell opened his boxes. They were crammed with similar tin holders, but with the difference that each contained eight watches, all carefully packed in tissue paper. Because of the paper and the cloth covering there could be no rattling of the watches in a lively sea.

"Where did you get your holders, since they didn't come out on the yacht?" Edgley asked.

"That was rather a headache at first," Furnell answered. "I couldn't get them from Baldwin lest the Customs people should examine them entering Switzerland and become interested. So I had them made here, the tins, I mean. The cloth I stuck on myself."

"No questions asked?"

"I said they were for an experimental automatic café machine. I don't know whether that was believed, but no remarks were passed."

"That was good."

While speaking the men were pushing the full holders into the slots, taking care that each was hooked to the next, so as to be easily withdrawn when the time came. The empty holders were next packed in Furnell's boxes, and after some more talk and drinks they put out the lights and crept back to the stern. Furnell climbed down into his dinghy and with his boxes drifted silently away into the night. The great operation was complete!

Next day Loxton and Edgley worked really hard. First, they went up to a wharf for oil. Then every inch of the yacht was cleaned, the water tanks were washed out and refilled, and all brass work was polished. When they had finished, the *Komforta* looked as if she had just left the builder's yard. "We've told those people we were going to clean her up," Loxton remarked. "They must see that we've done it."

The two following days both men claimed as a holiday, agreeing that it was well earned. They lay on the sun deck and smoked and had long tramps ashore. Next morning they bade farewell to Kaiseraugst and returned to Basle. By nine the passengers were once more on board.

The run back to Ramsgate was very similar to the outward journey, except that owing to the current the speed was much higher. Also as far as possible they called at

PART 1: THE BITERS BITE

different places. Baden, Wurms, the ascent of the Drachenfels and Amsterdam were substituted for Coblenz, Mainz and Dordrecht. This was generally approved. In fact it all went very well, and before the Rolls Royce again claimed the passengers they had expressed satisfaction with the arrangements. By noon on the Saturday the yacht was once more at anchor off Dolbey's cottage.

For a reason which was not explained to Edgley nothing was done that night, but on Sunday night the scenes at Kaiseraugst were repeated, Dolbey playing Furnell's part. At 2.00 a.m. Loxton and Edgley waited in the stern, a small dinghy silently materialized at the companion steps, and three boxes were lifted aboard and carried to the deck cabin. This time the boxes contained empty holders, and these were changed for those with the watches. They had their chats and drinks and then Dolbey vanished with his costly cargo.

"What happens to them now?" Edgley asked as they returned to the saloon.

"You don't know," retorted Loxton, "and I only approximately. Dolbey and Baldwin have thought out the details. How Baldwin works the distribution I don't know, but Campion, his storekeeper, is in it too and helps him."

"Slack week for us?"

"I don't think." Loxton was scornful. "You lazy devil, Peter, what do you think you're for? You've got to get her cleaned and restocked for the next trip."

"What about you?"

"Same for me, as you know very well. Fuel, gas, motor overhaul. I've plenty to do."

"Everything complete for the next trip – except the passengers."

"That's where you're wrong, old man. Dolbey gave me a letter from Butler's. They've fixed us a party of four."

"My word, Dick, the thing's going! That's wonderful!"

"Nothing wonderful about it. We take them at a reduction to get the thing known."

"I suppose that's wise. Who are we getting?"

"Four men. I gather they're elderly and retired, but I don't know who they are."

Edgley yawned. "Time enough to worry about it in a week. I'm for the hay. What about you?"

Loxton, it appeared, held similar views, and a few minutes later silence reigned on the *Komforta*.

– 4 –

THE MARSHAM EXPEDITION

On the morning after Loxton, Edgley and Dolbey had relieved the *Komforta* of her load of watches, work was in progress in the study of Dr George Marsham of The Gables, near Folkestone. Dr Marsham was dictating and his secretary, Nancy Kelso, was precariously taking down his weighty words in her somewhat erratic shorthand.

Dr Marsham was the uncle of Valentine Dolbey about whom Loxton had spoken to Edgley. Crippled from arthritis, he had given up his Harley Street practice and had moved to the house found for him by Dolbey. Though his body was frail, his mind was robust and acutely active. He was now engaged in writing a book on some obscure problems of cardiotherapy, and Nancy's job was to collate his notes, look up authorities, and type the resultant paragraphs.

As she waited for him to put his ideas in order before delivering the pronouncement which was to form his next sentence, her thoughts went back to the change in her prospects which this job had brought about. Six months earlier she was almost in despair. Her mother had died just when she left school, leaving her, an only child, alone with her father. He had been a doctor, and his wish and her own had been that she also should study medicine. She had indeed completed two years of the course. Then her father had died, and she discovered that he had been living up to his income and that little capital remained for her. It was necessary that she should quickly find means to support herself. There was no chance of finishing her medical course, but she estimated that she had enough to keep her while learning shorthand and typing. But before she had finished her training her money had run out and the heartbreaking search for a job had begun.

She tried without success for shorthand-typist posts with commercial and legal firms, which she would have loathed. She answered advertisements for secretary-receptionists for doctors and dentists, which would have been better, though still not what she would have liked. In every case she had been turned down because of her speeds. Neither her shorthand nor typing was up to scratch. Both were sound: she was painstaking and accurate in all that she did, but both were much too slow. And then just as she began to fear that her lack of funds would drive her into some hateful "labouring" job, she read Dr Marsham's advertisement. "Wanted as secretary to live in: a shorthand-typist with some medical knowledge." Well, she had that. In answer to her application there was a note asking her to call and enclosing a couple of pounds for her expenses, for she had written from London. She had had an interview that left her almost sick with desire, then she had been told that if her references proved satisfactory she would hear further. "Bad times, these, you know, my dear," the doctor had said, though adding with a kindly chuckle, "but in your case I'm sure a mere matter of form."

When two days later she received a letter offering her a month's probation as secretary, she felt that it was too impossibly good to be true. Yet no other conclusion could

PART 1: THE BITERS BITE

be drawn from the note. Unless she made some perfectly appalling break she would be sure of the job for at least a month. Then it would be up to her. With any reasonable luck she would pass her test and the appointment would be confirmed.

The job had surpassed her most sanguine expectations. It was indeed magnificent, and for several reasons. First, she was to live in and be treated as one of the family. In some cases this might not have been an advantage, but in so charming a house with its admirable service and quiet happy atmosphere, it was a quite fascinating prospect. The members of the family who lived there permanently were delightful. The doctor seemed goodness personified and his niece, Julia Parratt, who ran the house, had been most friendly and pleasant. Dr Marsham's nephew, Valentine Dolbey, she did not care for so much, but he was away all day, and though at no time had he much to say to her, he was invariably polite. He was the son of Marsham's sister, who had married an Irish barrister practising in Dublin. There Dolbey had been brought up and there he had lived till a few years before, when he had got a job with a firm of engineers in Folkestone. Nancy in fact described all three to herself by that word which has almost disappeared from the language: they were gentlefolk, with all of the straightness and kindness and regard for the feelings of others which that meant.

As she weighed the prospect of gracious living at The Gables against that of the cheap lodgings and crowded cafés which were all she had lately been able to afford, and which with an office job would be all she could have hoped for, she had almost wept for joy. And when she compared the doctor, with his straight clean look and courtly manners, with some of the businessmen to whom she had applied and whom she had loathed at sight, her delight was intensified. Nothing, she told herself earnestly, would be too much to do to please these nice people. It was not only to hold her job – of course it was that – but it was more. Already she wished to pay back in some measure their trust and kindness.

The job itself fortunately was one which she believed she could do reasonably well. Her medical knowledge was sufficient for the technical part of the work, and as she could do the typing in her own time, speed was not essential. In addition, as her secretarial duties scarcely constituted a whole time job, she was glad to help Miss Parratt with some items of the domestic economy.

The Gables was a small though charming furnished house on rising ground on the outskirts of Folkestone. From the terrace and garden, small also but beautifully kept and sheltered from the north and east by a belt of trees, there was a fine extended view over the town and out to the sea beyond. There were four servants, the doctor's attendant and male nurse, Rawlins; Janet, the cook; Edith, house and parlour maid and Gedge, the gardener-chauffeur. The first was a sallow individual with dark shifty eyes, to whom Nancy took an immediate dislike. Afterwards she wondered if she had misjudged him, for he had always been correct to her in manner. The others were cheerful and friendly and she got on excellently with all three.

Since this tremendous change in her life, Nancy had become almost a member of the family. She had made good at her job, in fact she had become rather more than a secretary. Not only had she frequently been sent to London to look up authorities and references, but she had on occasion acted as Dr Marsham's emissary in interviews with doctors and scientists. Primed with a list of the

PART 1: THE BITERS BITE

questions the doctor wished her to ask, she had in all cases been able to bring back adequate replies. She was on Christian name terms with Julia Parratt, and was now doing quite a considerable share of the housekeeping.

But these admirable features had one drawback, that of monotony. Indeed the only outstanding incident in the whole time was when Dolbey left The Gables. Dolbey she had come to regard as a rather queer fish. With him she seemed to have nothing in common. She hated to be left alone with him, as she never felt at ease and conversation between them quickly died. He was morose and discontented and apparently had a grudge against life. Julia Parratt had told her that he had been in the navy and had done well, and Nancy supposed his attitude was due to the comparative boredom of civilian life.

One evening when Nancy had been at The Gables for some three months she had happened to meet him on the drive as he was returning after his day's work. At once she noticed a change in him. He was walking more briskly and carrying himself better. The sulky look had vanished from his face and something like excitement showed in his eyes. He greeted her differently, not grudgingly, but as if he were glad to see her. All that evening he was in great form, though she thought he drank more than was good for him.

This continued for about a week, and then one evening at dinner he announced that he was leaving. "I'm after having a bit of luck," he explained. "I've met a fella and got him interested in my tide turbine, and he's agreed to put up the cash for some large scale experiments. I'm going over to work where there's a good run on the Stour."

"My dear fellow, that's first rate," Dr Marsham returned. "I'm delighted to hear it, though I'm sorry you'll be leaving here. But what about your job with the firm?"

"Ah, that's a wash-out altogether. I resigned three days ago."

"Rather sudden, isn't it, Val?" Julia put in. "You don't surely mean that you've left them for good?"

"Yes, my boy. You don't mean that you've given up a sure thing for what must necessarily be somewhat problematical?"

"I have indeed. Given the whole thing up. Sure what else could I do? The turbine'll take all the time I've got and more."

Dr Marsham seemed rather taken aback. "Well, of course you know what you're doing, but I always think it's a pity to throw out dirty water unless you've got clean to take its place."

Nancy could see that Dolbey was getting annoyed. "Haven't I clean in plenty to take its place?" he answered shortly: "the tide turbine. When once I get it going there'll be ten times the money in it than ever I'd get in Folkestone. Besides, amn't I sick to tears of the firm and everything connected with it."

The doctor seemed slightly offended. "Oh well," he said a little stiffly, "it's your business, not mine. Where do you propose to live?"

"On the Stour. I was over there today and I've got a little cottage." Dolbey spoke more politely.

"Lucky to get a cottage these days," Julia remarked. "Who'll look after you, Val?"

"Oh, I don't know. I'll try and get some local woman to come in and cook. If not, I can do it for myself the very best. We learn that in the service."

"Can you do experimenting like that single-handed?" the doctor inquired.

PART 1: THE BITERS BITE

"I can, or most of it anyway." Dolbey was now genial. "I've already bought two small scows I found in Dover Harbour. I'll get a tow to fetch 'em round to the Stour. I'll anchor them side by side and hang the turbine between them."

"It sounds heavy work."

"Ah, it's not all that heavy. You can do a lot with pulleys and shearlegs. Besides, the chap who's backing me will be there on and off and he'll give me a hand."

"I declare I'm getting quite interested. I'd like to drive over and see you when you get going."

"And why not, uncle? There's nothing I'd like better."

Two days after this exchange Dolbey departed. He came back at intervals, reporting that his invention was making satisfactory progress.

Today this episode was recalled to Nancy's mind by a sudden suggestion from the doctor. "I think that's enough for the present," he said, putting down his notes. "I'm tired of work and I'm sure you are too. What about taking a half holiday and going to see Val's turbine?"

"Oh," returned Nancy, "if you mean that I may come too, I'd love it."

"Well, naturally you must come too. What would I do if I got a sudden inspiration and you weren't there to take it down?"

Nancy laughed happily and he went on: "We'll make a party; I dare say Julia will join in. We might take lunch and picnic on the way. Will you see to it?"

Julia Parratt was willing and they packed provisions, while Gedge contentedly left his gardening and got out the rather ancient Daimler. It was always an effort for Dr Marsham to get into or out of a car. He could walk fairly well with two sticks, but the turning and getting into the seat he found more difficult. Fortunately the lugubrious Rawlins had the knack of helping him, which explained why the doctor would go nowhere without him.

Just past Dover they took a side road to where there was a fine view of the sea, and there they lunched. About three they reached the Stour, and following the directions Dolbey had given, arrived at his cottage. Tyre tracks showed that a building at the side which looked like a coach-house was now used as a garage. Under the same roof was an extension and from this issued sounds of hammering.

Investigation revealed this room as a carpenter's workshop and Dolbey as the carpenter. He seemed both surprised and pleased to see them.

"A sudden idea came to me this morning that I'd like an afternoon out and I remembered your kind invitation," Dr Marsham explained. "We sent a telegram, but perhaps you have not yet received it?"

"Ah, sure what did you bother about a telegram for?" Dolbey answered, "and anyway I haven't got it yet. I'm only too pleased to see you all. There," he pointed to his scows, "is the mighty work."

"How is it going?"

"Doing the best. It's generating at the present minute, but not so strongly as I want it to. You'll have to come out and give it the once over."

"I'd like to." The old man's eyes swept the reach. He nodded towards the *Komforta*, which was moored ahead of the scows. "That's a fine launch."

"She's all that and more. I've been over her. She belongs to a fella named Loxton. I was glad to make his acquaintance for he pays me for the privilege of mooring here and using my slip. He takes people on trips. But come in and see my mansion and sample my coffee."

PART 1: THE BITERS BITE

They declined the coffee, but said that if a cup of tea should materialize before they started home, it would be appreciated. After some talk Dolbey again suggested a visit to his scows.

"Thank you, Rawlins and I will go," the doctor answered.

While they were away Nancy and Julia sat and chatted, then after research among Dolbey's somewhat dubious culinary effects, made tea. By the time it was ready the others had returned.

The doctor was full of the turbine. "Well worth coming over to see," he told them. "Very ingenious, but I'm afraid rather hard work." Then seeing the cups, "Oh, a pleasant surprise. I wasn't expecting tea so soon."

"It's a pleasant surprise to me too," Dolbey asserted politely. "I never mind anyone doing my work for me."

"I'm sure we'd all like to go over that beautiful yacht," Dr Marsham went on. "It seems she's locked up, but the owner's expected any moment and Val says he'll show her to us. I must say I'd like a cruise in a boat like that."

"Well, wouldn't he be the pleased boy to take you?" Dolbey considered. "He runs trips up the Rhine, so he told me, though I gathered he's not tied to any special itinerary. Oh, there he is."

Dolbey went to the door and gave a hail, presently returning with Loxton. "And here's the lucky owner himself," he explained as he introduced him.

"We might some time be interested in your venture, Mr Loxton," Marsham went on, "and I wondered whether we might take the opportunity of being here to see over the ship?"

"Nothing I'd like better, except perhaps," Loxton smiled, "to book you for a cruise. But I'm afraid the dinghy's rather small, so if you don't mind we'll make two trips. You'll come, Dolbey?"

"I will indeed. I'd like to."

"Then shall we take the ladies first, sir, and come back for you and your man?"

"No," put in Julia. "You and Rawlins go first, uncle, and while the boat's away we'll wash up the tea things."

This was agreed to in spite of Dolbey's protests. With considerable difficulty Dr Marsham was helped into the dinghy and then on to the *Komforta*'s deck. Dolbey had gone out with them and he brought the dinghy back, while Loxton remained on the yacht to do the honours. Having left a clean kitchen, the ladies were soon aboard.

Nancy was immensely taken with the *Komforta*. Though she knew little about boats, she had admired from the bank her sturdy appearance and trim lines. When she reached the deck she was still more pleased with the large clear space, the first rate fittings and the spotless cleanliness of everything.

But it was not till she went below that she reached her climax of admiration. The state rooms with their soft beds and shaded reading lamps, the nearby bathroom, and the two saloons with their comfortable chairs enchanted her, and she thought that the handsome panelling, soft carpets and pretty curtains set off admirably the well-selected furniture.

It was therefore with a growing thrill that she listened to Dr Marsham's talk with Loxton. "I admire your yacht very much," he was saying. "I'd like to know more of your plans. Val said you ran trips up the Rhine. How far do you go?"

"Basle as a rule," Loxton answered. "But our idea is not to offer a cut and dried programme. We can do so if it's

PART 1: THE BITERS BITE

desired of course. But if we get a party we want to go wherever the party likes. I mean of course in reason."

"If I were interested at all," the doctor went on, "it would be as an easy way of getting to Switzerland. I find gangways and platforms and crowds and the high steps of Continental trains are rather too much for me and unhappily flying makes me ill. But if I could step on board your yacht here and stay put till we reached Basle it would be a different matter."

"Nothing easier, sir. Dolbey mentioned that you lived near Folkestone. You could either come aboard like the others at Ramsgate, or if you preferred, we could run down and pick you up at Folkestone."

"That would certainly be convenient. And at Basle?"

"At Basle we come alongside a small wharf actually in the town and you could go ashore there."

"That sounds satisfactory also."

"Is it Basle you wish to visit?"

"No, as a matter of fact it's Zürich. But I would hire a car and have it meet your yacht."

"Zürich? Just let me look at the map. From Basle to Zürich by road is," he scaled rapidly, "about fifty miles. Is that too much for you?"

"Oh no, I don't think so."

"Because if it was, I think we could take the yacht further upstream. There's a little place called – let's see – Eglisau, and it seems to be only fifteen or sixteen miles from Zürich."

"Thank you for the suggestion. But fifty miles would not be too much for me. Indeed, once I'm in the car, a few miles extra makes little difference."

"I see. Then I think Basle would suit admirably. The car could be at the wharf."

"Excellent. Now another point. How long would I have ashore?"

"That rather depends on how many stops you want to make on the way there and back."

"I shouldn't want to make any. I should ask for a quick passage each way."

"Well, let's count up. Our normal trip lasts four weeks. We couldn't prolong it much beyond that, for we have to prepare the yacht for the next trip which is advertised for a definite sailing date. We should take eight or nine days each way for the journeys. That would leave you ten or eleven days in Switzerland."

"That would suit me admirably."

"You could do it comfortably."

" 'Pon my word, the prospect is very tempting. What do you say, Julia? Would you care for it?"

Julia laughed. "Why, uncle, I'd just love it! I can't imagine anything I'd like better."

"And you, Nancy? I should want you in Zürich. It's to see Professor Dahlmann, as I expect you've guessed."

Professor Dahlmann was a world authority on the diseases of the heart and their treatment, and the two men had been conducting a somewhat desultory correspondence on certain matters to be treated of in Dr Marsham's book. Often the doctor had complained about the unsatisfactory nature of letters, and wished he could have met his correspondent face to face. He had had several invitations from Dahlmann, but always the difficulty of the journey had put him off.

Nancy grew excited at the thought of herself taking part in the excursion. Her continental wanderings had consisted of two short visits to Paris, and apart from travelling in this lovely yacht, the prospect of seeing a little of Germany and

PART 1: THE BITERS BITE

Switzerland was alluring. She expressed her feelings in a suitably restrained, though quite unmistakeable fashion.

"You two would have to share a cabin," Marsham went on. "Rawlins could come in with me. That all right, Mr Loxton? Or is it Captain Loxton?"

Loxton laughed. "You don't require to give me either handle, sir. But I find Captain goes down better when dealing with harbour-masters and so on."

"Very right. Well, it seems that I only want information on two other matters: first, what dates are still open and second, the rather important one of costs. Perhaps you would let me have a statement of those to consider when I reach home."

"With pleasure, sir. I'll get it out for you with a detailed itinerary."

The following day the letter came. The normal charge, it appeared, was £30 per head per week, which for the four weeks would come to £480. But on this occasion, without excursions and seeing the yacht would be lying up so long in Switzerland, it would be possible to make a substantial reduction. The whole trip could be done for £300, of which £180 would be spent in England. The foreign cost would therefore be only £120, and as there was permission to spend £100 per head, this would leave the party £280 for their expenses in Switzerland. As to dates, the four-week period from Saturday, 15th June to 13th July was still available. Loxton hoped he would have the pleasure of meeting the party on this trip, but as he was next day leaving for the Rhine, he would be grateful if Dr Marsham would kindly reply to Messrs Butler of Cockspur Street.

Nancy scarcely dared to breathe while Marsham was digesting this information, then delight surged up in her mind as he dictated a letter to Professor Dahlmann asking could they meet during the period in question. When further a cordial reply arrived from Dahlmann, expressing pleasure at the prospect and inviting the party to stay with him, she found it hard to control her excitement. It was with the deepest satisfaction that she typed a letter to Messrs Butler making a definite booking and enclosing a cheque to seal the transaction. It was further arranged that the yacht would call at Folkestone to embark the party.

For the next month the days could not pass quickly enough for Nancy, but the slow process of time at last brought the momentous Saturday. What a pleasure it was to her packing her own things, and what thought and care she gave to the selection of the doctor's papers which were to be taken! And then towards six in the evening, looking down over the town, what a thrill it was to see the *Komforta* approach and slowly enter the harbour! Half an hour later the telephone rang: Loxton to say that the dinghy was waiting at the steps. The moment had arrived.

It had been arranged that on this first night they should dine on the yacht, as Marsham felt that they could settle down more comfortably by going then rather than merely in time for bed. Gedge, who lived close by, was to drive them down, return the car, and look after the garden while they were away. Edith and Janet had been given a month's leave, during which time the house would be shut up.

Loxton in a blue semi-naval uniform was waiting for them at the steps, and with him was another man also in uniform whom he briefly introduced as "Edgley; purser, steward, cabin attendant, cook and general stand-by in case of need." Fine looking men both were, Nancy thought. Loxton indeed was rather handsome and obviously capable, though perhaps not too good tempered. Edgley was less spectacular, but gave an impression of greater kindliness and approachability.

Embarkation took only a few minutes and soon they were unpacking in their respective cabins. Then came dinner, and as Edgley had been earlier, so now the whole party was charmed with the table: the spotless linen, the glittering silver and glass, and the carefully arranged flowers. The food also was excellent and admirably cooked. Over coffee Marsham announced his opinion: "A good beginning! If they keep this up we won't do so badly." The sentiments were also Nancy's, but it was not the way she would have expressed hers.

The evening was mild and after dinner they moved to the sun deck, where first Loxton and later Edgley joined them. The talk turned to the Rhine and what was to be seen along it, and Loxton explained that since the doctor would be satisfied with ten days in Zürich, it would be possible, if they so desired, to stop for half-days at Cologne, Coblenz and Mainz. Marsham at once agreed, though Nancy was sure he did not personally wish it, but did so to enable Julia and her to see a little of the country. It would, she felt, be just like him. Even to her, his paid assistant, his thought was always, what would she like?

She was too excited to sleep immediately on going to bed, and Julia also being wakeful, they read till the small hours. Then at last Nancy dropped off. When she again became drowsily conscious there was an unusual muffled throbbing going on beneath her and her bed was swaying gently. Then suddenly wide awake, she sprang up and went to a porthole. Outside the sun was shining on a sea of almost incredible cleanness, dark blue flecked with white, while close to the porthole a foam-crested wave raced by.

ANYTHING TO DECLARE?

Julia waking at the same time, they put on dressing-gowns and went on deck. It was a perfect morning. The sun was warm and the slight breeze was behind them, so that they scarcely felt it. They were creeping along the coast, with Dover some five miles away to port. In all directions were ships passing up and down the Straits. Presently Loxton saw them and waved from the wheelhouse.

"You've brought us luck," he called. "We've never yet had such a crossing. There's a good forecast and we'll get it calm all the way."

His promise was fulfilled and for most of the day they basked in easy chairs on the sun deck. Then in the afternoon a faint low line of coast came into view to starboard. They moved up along this, till shortly before dinner they dropped anchor off Flushing.

"That's all for today," Loxton declared as he left the wheelhouse. "We lie here till the morning, partly to give you an undisturbed night, but also because your terribly overworked captain and crew would themselves like a spot of sleep."

Next day they advanced through the islands and into the Rhine proper, passing towards evening under the great Moerdijk bridges and lying up near the little town of Gorinchen. On second thoughts Dr Marsham had decided to push on to Basle without pause, in case his conferences took longer than he had anticipated. He would leave Zürich as soon as he had finished, and any sight-seeing there was then time for could be done on the downward journey.

Accordingly each day from morning till evening they fought their way upstream against the strong current. Though to Nancy all the trip was delightful, its interest varied from mile to mile. Progress on the flat lower reaches seemed to drag, but places like the Drachenfels and the

PART 1: THE BITERS BITE

Lorelei Rock hurried past far too quickly. She looked with longing at the towns, so clean and tidy, so obviously prosperous and so full of trees, and as they forged endlessly on, she hoped for time to visit them on the way back.

Sailing by day and lying up by night, they reached Basle just after lunch on the eighth day. Loxton had arranged for a car to meet them, and the necessary deposit having been paid, the driver handed it over to the party and disappeared. Rawlins had driven in the war, and he was to act as chauffeur as well as attending to Dr Marsham.

Nancy enjoyed every minute of their two-hour drive to Zürich through the pleasant country and the spotless villages. It was all *foreign* and except for Paris it was her first trip abroad. Even driving on the wrong side of the road was a thrill. Then Zürich and their fine hotel on the Quai overlooking the lake, for Professor Dahlmann's invitation had not been accepted. As she gazed from her room out over the water and watched a steamer tying up at the nearby wharf, she felt that the next ten days would fall no whit behind those that had already passed.

It was after dinner on that first night in Zürich that a small jar disturbed the smooth running which till then had marked the expedition. After finishing the two cigarettes Dr Marsham allowed himself with his coffee, he went to his private sitting room to go over his papers for the interview with Professor Dahlmann on the next morning. Presently his voice was heard calling Nancy.

"I can't find my notes on the agenda for tomorrow's meeting," he explained when she entered. "Were they in the case?"

"Yes, they're there somewhere. I distinctly remember seeing them when I checked over before we left the launch."

"Well, I can't find them. I wish you'd have a look."

"They were in tomorrow's folder." As Nancy spoke she lifted all papers out of the attaché case and laid them on the table. Then examining each, she replaced it in the case.

"They're rather important," Marsham went on as she worked. "Figures and formulae. They're things one can't remember and there'd be no use in our meeting without them."

"I know the papers," she answered. "But they're here: they must be."

"Well, I hope so, for it would take three or four days to work out new figures and we just haven't the time." He watched her anxiously till she replaced the last paper. "You don't see them?"

"I don't," she declared in a puzzled tone, "but I know they're here. I stacked all the papers on the table in the saloon ready for packing and I'm quite positive the notes were among them. Then I lifted the whole lot into the case."

He looked at her anxiously. "You left the saloon between checking them over and putting them in the case?"

"Did I?" Nancy considered. "Yes, I did. Julia called me to discuss something about our luggage, but I wasn't away many minutes."

Marsham's face assumed an expression of distress. "It must have been during those minutes," he declared. "Look, Nancy, I've just remembered. I'm the culprit. I wanted to refresh my memory on a point and I saw the notes in your pile and took them to the deck saloon. I was reading them when Edgley looked in to say we were entering Basle. I laid them down on the settee and went out on the sun deck. There I got interested in our progress and forgot all about them."

PART 1: THE BITERS BITE

"Oh, Dr Marsham, I'm so sorry. I should have checked them again."

"My dear child, what nonsense! You're not to blame. You've done everything admirably and the fault was entirely mine."

"You're very good, but I feel guilty."

"Well, you mustn't. Now the question is, what had we better do? Would you mind very much going back for them tomorrow morning and we'll put the professor off till the afternoon?"

"Of course I'd go. But," she hesitated, "I seem to remember that Professor Dahlmann said he was engaged in the afternoons. Did he not say that he went to the hospital in the morning and would take his leave during your visit, but in the afternoon he saw private patients?"

Marsham nodded sadly. "I'm afraid you're right. Then it means that we lose a day. Very unfortunate, but we can't help it. Then there's no hurry about your trip: any time tomorrow will do."

Nancy was thinking. "I wonder if we couldn't do better?" she said. "It's not quite ten yet. Supposing we were to go now, for I suppose Rawlins would drive me. We could get to the launch by midnight and be back here by two. That would save your day and no one would be any the worse."

At first he wouldn't hear of it, but Nancy persisted and gradually he gave way. But under no circumstances would he allow her to go off alone with Rawlins. "Rawlins suits me all right," he declared, "but sometimes there's a look in his eye that I don't like. But as far as that goes I expect Julia would go with you."

They discussed it and then Nancy had a further idea. Why need either of them go? Surely Rawlins could do all that was wanted? If at the worst he should fail, Nancy could go next day. In that case they'd be no worse off than they were at present.

Finally, this was agreed on. After some difficulty Rawlins was found and the matter explained to him. He had no objection whatever to the run and saw no difficulty in getting the papers. Delighted to have thus justified her existence, Nancy saw him off. The clocks were striking eleven as he drove out of the hotel yard.

– 5 –

THE CHINK IN THE ARMOUR

If Nancy Kelso was enjoying the trip, so also in his somewhat grudging way was Joseph Rawlins. Before the war he had been an attendant in a large mental hospital and compared to that his work for the doctor was child's play. At Folkestone he had an easy time and good money, but there wasn't enough to keep him occupied and he was bored. This Swiss visit was therefore a welcome break.

He was interested in the journey for another reason. Finding the work at the mental hospital both exacting and distressing, he had volunteered for the army on the outbreak of war. For their own good reasons the military authorities had decided his nursing experience would give him a useful background of mechanical knowledge, and he had accordingly been trained as a lorry driver. After service in the Middle East he had landed in Normandy some weeks after D-day, and had driven his lorry to Holland with the advancing columns. Later he had on different occasions been backwards and forwards across the Rhine, and he was now thrilled to see from a different angle the places at which he had crossed.

He had never before been in Switzerland, but by ten on that first night he had decided that he was going to enjoy the country. With the smattering of German he had picked up and the English spoken by so many of the citizens, he was able to make himself understood everywhere. Already he had found a little garden on the shores of the lake where the most excellent beer was to be obtained. Apparently, moreover, he was going to have a good deal of free time and he felt that he would have no difficulty in spending it satisfactorily.

This feeling was somewhat dashed when about half past ten an hotel servant found him and told him that his services were in demand, and he was considerably disgruntled when he learnt that instead of the comfortable bed he had been looking forward to, he had to drive through half the night. Just what one might expect, he thought pessimistically. When things begin to look good a snag always turns up to cheat one out of the benefit.

All the same he took Nancy's instructions with a good grace, said he was sure he would have no difficulty in finding the papers, accepted with thanks the thermos of coffee and the sandwiches she had prepared for him, and drove off with a respectful smile.

It was a fine night, dry and clear and with some light from a crescent moon. In a strange country he played safe and drove slowly. True he had been over the road once before, but in the opposite direction and by lamplight it looked entirely different. It was of course clearly signposted and he had no trouble in finding his way.

He kept on the main Basle road till a few miles from the city, then finding a turning marked "Kaiseraugst", he took it. It was after one when be reached the village.

At once he found himself up against a difficulty he had not foreseen. The launch, Loxton had said, would be lying near Kaiseraugst and he had thought that he could not fail to find it immediately. But now he realized that the word "near" was an elastic term. The *Komforta* might be tied up

PART 1: THE BITERS BITE

opposite any one of a number of little piers or wharfs on a longish reach. He could think of only one thing to do. Parking the car, he left it and began to walk down the bank.

This in itself was neither rapid nor easy, for much of the ground was private property. To his great distaste he had to trespass across garden after garden. His principal fear was dogs, for if he were discovered he would find it difficult to explain his presence. Apart from dogs there would, he felt sure, be officials about, for the river being an international boundary, it would undoubtedly be watched day and night. However he persevered, for some time without success. Then at last he reaped his reward.

He had gone down to a small wharf in some rather extensive grounds, and finding nothing there, had walked to the boundary in the hope of observing the next property. It was a small place, just a cottage surrounded by a garden. On the bank was a boatslip to which a skiff was tied.

Disappointed, he glanced out over the river and then felt a wave of satisfaction. Moored in the stream was a large launch, and though he could not see her name he had no doubt from her silhouette that she was the *Komforta*.

Now a new problem presented itself. How could he without waking the entire neighbourhood attract Loxton's attention? Both men would be below and probably asleep and would not hear any but the loudest calls. Before he aroused them he would have the people of the surrounding houses out to see what was wrong.

His thoughts turned to the skiff. To borrow it would solve the problem, but it was unlikely that it contained sculls, and without them he dared not push it out lest he should miss the launch.

He was about to climb the fence to find out if sculls were available when he saw a movement in the next garden.

ANYTHING TO DECLARE?

Instantly he crouched behind a shrub. It was a man and he was walking towards the slip. Rawlins could see him only dimly in the moonlight. He was moving silently and carrying something which appeared to be heavy. He reached the slip, put down his burden and returned like a shadow to the cottage, disappearing round its corner to the rear.

Rawlins was interested, but it looked as if the operation, whatever it was, was incomplete. Investigation, he felt, would be ill-timed. The event proved him correct. Before long the man appeared for the second time, carrying a load apparently similar to the first. This also he laid on the slip.

If Rawlins up till now had been intrigued, the man's subsequent movements thrilled him. He drew the skiff up to the slip and made it fast fore and aft. Then embarking, he cautiously lifted in three obviously heavy objects. Rawlins could not see what they were, but they looked like boxes or parcels of some kind.

The cargo stowed, the man cast off and with a pair of sculls began to row. He had to head almost directly upstream, but gradually the skiff moved out from the bank till at last it was lost in shadow against the *Komforta*'s side. All then became motionless and silent.

At least not completely silent, for the movement of the great body of water made its own peculiar noise: a sort of soft rushing bourdon with sounds of the breaking of tiny waves and the swirling of dissolving eddies. There were little plops and splashes also, probably water rats or other small animals. Ordinary noises from the launch Rawlins would have heard above the river, but on board all remained dark and still.

Rawlins also remained silent and motionless. He was thinking deeply. What could be happening that required to be done in the dead of night, silently and without lights?

PART 1: THE BITERS BITE

Normally the boatman would have given a hail and the *Komforta* would have switched on a deck lamp. The whole operation of the transport of the packages would thus have been eased. Some strong reason prevented it.

That reason obviously was secrecy. Something was being taken aboard the launch about which no outsider must know. What could it be?

Something illegal surely. What else could account for such careful precautions? Then an idea flashed into Rawlins' mind and a sudden excitement filled his entire being.

If something illegal was going on and he could find out what it was, might it not mean money? Might it not mean even wealth? If it was worth all the trouble that was being taken it must be valuable, and if so Loxton and Edgley would certainly pay to have it kept secret.

Though pretty hard bitten, Rawlins was not exactly dishonest. If he saw a chance of profit he would usually take it without worrying overmuch about its ethics, but he would not deliberately cheat or steal. But blackmail he did not consider dishonest. It was simply a commercial transaction. You had something of value and you sold it. And why not? If the other chap didn't want it he wouldn't buy. All perfectly fair and above board.

Under normal circumstances Rawlins might have reasoned differently, but his circumstances at this time were not normal. Some six months previously the Marsham's housemaid had left. It had not been easy to replace her, but at last Miss Parratt had found a substitute. Edith Jones was a younger woman, good looking, efficient, pleasant mannered: in Rawlins' eyes in fact, eminently desirable. He had promptly fallen for her. He had asked her to marry him, intending that they should settle down as man and wife in the doctor's or some other service. But Edith had other ideas. She wanted a pub. If Rawlins could supply her with a pub which they could run jointly, she would marry him. Otherwise she would look elsewhere. So it was that above all else Rawlins wanted money. It followed that if there were any chances in what he had seen, he would be a fool to neglect them.

In the meantime there was nothing he could do but watch, and he grew slowly colder and stiffer as he remained crouching behind his shrub. It was clear that if the affair was to be kept secret the boatman would move the skiff away from the *Komforta* before it grew light. He must therefore come ashore during darkness, and Rawlins decided that this was something he must see. He might indeed get closer and see better. Silently he climbed the fence and took up his position behind another shrub, this time on the boatman's ground near the slip. He had been careful to tread only on grass and was satisfied that he had left no footprints.

Time began to drag and he grew even colder and stiffer. He could see from the illuminated figures on his wristwatch that it was now after three. Then with a shock of anger at his own carelessness he took off the watch and dropped it into his pocket. Its faint radiance might easily have been seen by the unknown.

It must, Rawlins afterwards calculated, have been after four when a shadow detached itself from the *Komforta*'s side and began to approach the slip. Again the boatman made no sound. Rawlins had been standing upright to ease the strain on his legs and now he crouched down again, watching intently.

The former proceedings were reversed. The skiff closed with the bank and was made fast bow and stern. Its occupant lifted three objects on to the slip, then stepping

PART 1: THE BITERS BITE

out himself, caught up one of the objects and walked with it to the cottage.

"Now for a better look," thought Rawlins. The man had no sooner disappeared than he stepped quickly forward, went out on the slip, and stooped to examine the remaining objects. They were, he quickly saw, wooden boxes some foot square by six inches deep, with a lock on the lid and handles on opposite sides.

He would have liked to examine them more closely, but on the outward journey the man had not spent long in the cottage and Rawlins thought he should get back into cover without delay. He was just in time. As he crouched down once more behind his shrub the man approached. He carried away the second box, returned for the third, and then vanished. The activity, whatever it was, seemed over for the night.

Rawlins now had two problems to solve. The most important – what these people were doing and how he could turn it to his advantage – could wait, but the other must be dealt with at once: what should be his own next move?

It was obvious that under no circumstances must Loxton and his friends suspect that he had learnt of their operations. It was equally clear that he must obtain the doctor's papers and deliver them to him before ten that morning.

He made his way back to the car while considering the matter. If he left Kaiseraugst by eight he should be back in Zürich before ten. It would take some time to get aboard the launch and perhaps longer still to find the papers, so he should be at the cottage not later than seven. The Swiss were early people and the man would certainly be up. It was now just after four, so he had nearly three hours to wait. He ate his sandwiches, rolled himself in a rug, and went to sleep.

A couple of hours later he awoke considerably refreshed and at seven he drove to the cottage. It looked a pleasant little place, partly creeper covered and with, as he had already seen, an admirably kept garden. A tall stoutly built young man opened to his knock.

Rawlins began by apologizing for the early call in his halting German, but the man interrupted him. "Are you English by any chance?" he asked. "If so, I speak the language."

"That makes it easier for me, sir," Rawlins smiled. "As you have heard, I'm not good at German."

"Oh, I understood you perfectly. Now what can I do for you?"

"I wanted to ask, sir, if I could get aboard the launch which is lying off your ground? As perhaps you know, it brought Dr Marsham and party to Switzerland. I'm Dr Marsham's attendant," and he went on to tell about the papers.

The tale did not suffer in the telling. It appeared that the doctor was a martyr to insomnia. He had been awake that morning in the early hours, and to pass the time he had decided to look over some papers dealing with his meeting with Professor Dahlmann. He had been unable to find them and at last remembered that he had left them aboard the *Komforta*. As without them his interview with the professor would have been useless, he had roused Rawlins and asked him if he would mind driving over for them. Rawlins had left Zürich about five and here he was.

"Well," said the man on hearing all this, "that's easily fixed up. I don't know anything about the launch people except that they pay me for the use of my slip, but I have a boat down there and I can put you aboard."

PART 1: THE BITERS BITE

As they walked round the cottage and down to the river Rawlins saw that this remark in itself practically established the illegality of the operations. The young man gave a stentorian hail, "Launch ahoy!" and Loxton's head presently appeared.

"Good morning," he called back, then seeing Rawlins, "Oh, hullo, Mr Rawlins. This is unexpected. Nothing wrong, I hope?"

Rawlins briefly explained.

"Then come aboard and have a look. Can you let him use your boat, Furnell?"

"Of course."

Rawlins did not know of the experiences of Alice's Red Queen, but he found, as far as the skiff was concerned, that he had to row quite hard to keep in the same place. As he pulled, the skiff edged across the gap and he was soon tied up at the *Komforta*'s companion.

"Papers?" said Loxton as he stepped aboard. "I did see papers in the deck saloon after you had gone ashore. I put them in the settee in case they might be valuable. Come and see if they're what you want. How did the doctor stand the drive to Zürich?"

"Surprisingly well, Captain Loxton. Quite fresh on arrival and everything satisfactory till he missed his papers. It seems they're chemical details and so on, and without them he and the professor would have had nothing to discuss."

"Well, here are what I found at all events. Are these right?"

Rawlins examined the papers, which exactly met Nancy's description. "Yes, these are they and thank you very much."

"When did you have a meal?" went on Loxton. "What about a spot of breakfast?"

"I had some sandwiches in the car after I started, but if you're having breakfast a cup of coffee would come in very handy."

"Sit down for five minutes and it'll be ready."

Certainly there was nothing in Loxton's manner nor in his greeting to the occupant of the cottage – whose name appeared to be Furnell – to suggest illegal nocturnal activities. Nor on this unexpected visit to the launch could Rawlins see anything in the slightest degree unusual or suggestive. On the plea of wanting a wash he went below, and as the other two were forward, had a peep into the cabins, including Loxton's. But he could find no trace of the boxes or of any objects which they might have contained.

During breakfast they chatted normally and then Rawlins rowed himself ashore, expressed his thanks to Furnell, and started back to Zürich. It was now light and he drove fast. As the clocks struck ten he walked into the hotel. He rang through at once to Nancy. "Just to tell you the doctor may make his mind easy, miss. I've got the papers. Sorry for being so late, but I was delayed. I'll tell you afterwards."

During the drive Rawlins had been considering how it came about that he was so late, and when the doctor asked him he was therefore able to account for it. "I missed the way somehow last night, sir," he explained: "took the wrong road in the dark. The roads are signposted all right, but of course the signs are not lit up and I must have driven past the post without seeing it. It took me quite a while to get back on the right road. Then I had a bit of trouble finding the *Komforta*," and he offered a circumstantial account of his difficulties. "By the time I saw her it was getting on to five. I didn't know how to attract Captain Loxton's

PART 1: THE BITERS BITE

attention without waking up the neighbourhood, so I decided to rest in the car till about seven, when he would be about."

Dr Marsham, happy with his notes, was not unduly interested. He regretted politely that Rawlins had had so much trouble and the incident was closed.

The stay in Zürich passed quickly to Rawlins, as he had a good deal of spare time and soon learnt how to enjoy it. During the morning visits to Professor Dahlmann he had to be in attendance, but Dr Marsham usually rested during the afternoon, and then Rawlins was free. He was sorry for Nancy, who was not only present at the interviews, but seemed to have to type all the afternoon and evening as well. He gathered that the visit was a success and that Dr Marsham had obtained the information he required, whatever it was.

Just ten days after they arrived the business was completed. All the discussions had taken place, they had had a number of fine excursions in the car, and Professor Dahlmann had assured them that on his first leave he would come over and see England, making the house at Folkestone his headquarters. After lunch on that day Rawlins drove out of the hotel courtyard for the last time. Two hours later they were aboard the *Komforta* at Basle. While they were having tea Loxton cast off and they began slipping rapidly down the Rhine towards home.

The voyage back was uneventful except for two full afternoon excursions ashore. On both occasions the doctor made himself comfortable on the sun deck and Rawlins was invited to join the others. He much enjoyed these trips as well as the journey as a whole. But pleasure seeking was not his main concern. The mysterious boxes! Could he find where they were on board, or, if they had been taken ashore again at Kaiseraugst, what had happened to their contents? During the week's run he managed with the greatest caution to examine the entire ship. When all were on deck or forward he searched the after cabins. When Edgley was helping Loxton to moor to a buoy or tie up at a wharf he went forward to Edgley's cabin and the galley. During the passage when Loxton was steering and Edgley preparing dinner in the galley he penetrated to the engine room. At one time or another he investigated every open space with the most minute care. And all for nothing. He could find no trace of anything which should not be there.

In due course they reached Folkestone, went ashore, and their former life at The Gables was resumed. Rawlins' problem remained unsolved while at the same time it grew more pressing than ever. Edith still agreed that if he could produce a pub she would marry him, but now she hinted not too obscurely that unless he hurried up and achieved some result, her undertaking would lapse.

As time passed he grew increasingly exasperated. He believed that he had at his hand the key to the situation, and yet he could not grasp it. If only he had been able to find out what the *Komforta* people were doing, he would by this time have had the cash for the pub and maybe a useful annual income as well. By the hour he pondered over the problem and for the hundredth time he asked himself why he had failed to discover the nature of the racket. Rather despairingly he wondered whether it was too late to try again.

Then one day an idea shot into his mind and he sat rigid, lost in the dawning hope that perhaps at long last he had grasped the illusive key.

– 6 –

THE SURE WINNER

The more Rawlins considered his new idea, the more obvious and satisfactory it seemed. Now indeed what puzzled him most was why he had not thought of it sooner. Where, he asked himself, had he visited another layout like Furnell's cottage at Kaiseraugst?

His mind went back to the doctor's excursion to see Dolbey and his turbine. There close to the bank of the Stour the *Komforta* had lain at anchor. There was the cottage, the boatslip, the young man living alone. There, he was now certain, took place the complementary operation to that he had witnessed. The illicit objects loaded up at the one were beyond doubt put ashore at the other.

If so, it explained a matter which at the time had mildly puzzled him. At Folkestone Dolbey had always seemed discontented, fed up with life in general and his job in particular. Then one evening after a visit to London he had come in excited and in excellent spirits, shortly after which he had thrown up his job and gone to this cottage on the Stour. Ostensibly this was to work at his tide turbine, which work he said someone had financed.

Now Rawlins wondered if the tide turbine was a blind to cover his help with the game the *Komforta* people were playing. Was it about this game that he had learnt on that visit to London? The fact that the Rhine trips began shortly after his move gave strong colour to the view.

Then Rawlins hugged himself. If he were right, it was not too late for further investigation. The money might still be within his grasp.

It was part of his job to tidy Dr Marsham's study, and one morning while the old man was still in bed he made a search among his papers. Presently he found what he wanted. It was a folder of the *Komforta*'s cruises. He took it from its drawer and slipped it into his pocket.

He saw that the launch was due to reach Ramsgate at the conclusion of its present cruise late on the Friday week, in twelve days' time. It anchored in the harbour and its passengers went ashore on Saturday morning, when presumably it moved to the Stour. On the following Saturday it left for another trip. No doubt it lay at Dolbey's for the week, during which it must unload the illegal Swiss articles. Rawlins thought that with luck he might witness the operation.

It happened that he was due a week's holidays and that very day he asked Marsham if he could take them during the critical period. The doctor agreed and Rawlins set to work to think out his plan.

Two days later on his afternoon off he took a train to Ramsgate, arriving about four. He went to a garage and hired a small car for the week in question, putting down the necessary deposit so that he could drive it alone. Having bought a large scale map of the town and district, he took a bus to Sandwich to see as much as he could of the Stour area. Well pleased with his afternoon's work, he had supper and returned to Folkestone.

During the next few days he felt restless and excited, but fought hard not to show it. If Edith noticed anything she

PART 1: THE BITERS BITE

would ask questions, and he feared that to put her off would risk a complete breach between them. Yet he daren't tell her the truth: he daren't tell it to *anyone*. What he proposed was blackmail and blackmail was a serious crime. Moreover, if he discovered the launch party's game and didn't report it, he would automatically become an accessory after the fact. To tell Edith about it would make her an accessory also. That he dare not risk. All the same he could not refrain from giving her a hint that at last he was on to money. When she questioned him he told her he would know more about it when he returned from his holiday. Without actually committing herself she hinted that if the amount was satisfactory the question of marriage might be discussed.

At long last the fateful Saturday arrived. Eager and excited, he went by an afternoon train to Ramsgate. There he claimed his car. In a small hotel he engaged a room for a week, saying he would not be moving in till the next morning. Having stocked his car with provisions for the night, he waited till it was dusk, then drove to Dolbey's, where he parked along the road. Then passing down through the rough grass to the Stour, he selected a point of vantage and lay down to watch.

It was a charming night. There was a thin crescent moon and in the clear sky stars were already showing. Across a bend of the river he could dimly see Dolbey's cottage and the *Komforta* lying in her usual place ahead of the scows. Till it was quite dark he was safer at this distance from the cottage, but before operations started he must go nearer. To kill time he ate some sandwiches, then if he had not been so much interested, he could have slept.

He wondered what Dolbey would do with the stuff. If he kept whatever it was in his cottage all would be well. But suppose he drove it away somewhere in his car? That wouldn't be quite so simple.

Well, he would meet the difficulty when it arose. He lay down where he was till shortly before midnight. Then leaving his hiding place, he pushed his way into Dolbey's grounds and settled down behind a bush close to the slipway. From there he could see everything that went on and unless Dolbey had acquired a dog – and there was no sign of it – he would be secure.

The night continued fine and warm. The slight breeze which had been blowing earlier had died down. As on that other night some two months before when he had also watched beside a river, the crescent moon would enable him to see what took place. Except for the gentle lapping of water and the rumble of cars on the road, it was very still. Rawlins realized that if he were discovered he might be in some danger, but thoughts of Edith and the pub revived his courage.

At Kaiseraugst no move had been made till about two and Rawlins resigned himself to wait till that hour. But two came and nothing happened. It was now cold and he was growing stiff, but he could not afford to move. Still there was no sign.

A growing anxiety was now added to his physical discomfort. Had he been too late? Had the objects, whatever they were, gone ashore at Ramsgate? The *Komforta* had lain at anchor in the harbour during the night. Had some skiff visited her in the small hours? Or had the cases been put ashore during daylight when the yacht had arrived in the Stour?

Rawlins did not think so. Judging by the precautions he had seen at Kaiseraugst nothing would be done either in a

PART 1: THE BITERS BITE

busy harbour or by day. No, he believed the booty must still be on board.

But why had they not put it ashore during this Saturday night when everything favoured the operation? Rawlins could not tell, but it seemed certain that nothing would now be done. It was getting on to five and already a faint light was showing in the east. He might give up.

All the same he watched till six when the sun was shining. Then, weary and discouraged, he drove back to Ramsgate. He parked, waited about till eight, and returned to his hotel. After breakfast he lay down and had a sleep.

Slowly the Sunday dragged away and by dark he was once again behind his shrub at Dolbey's. Again the same weary vigil began, but this time there was a difference. One had scarcely chimed on some distant clock when he heard a faint sound: a door had been opened. Presently there were steps and Dolbey appeared moving silently towards the slip. He was carrying something and Rawlins believed it was a case some foot square by six inches deep.

Dolbey put his burden down on the slip and went quietly back to the house. Rawlins, tense from excitement, timed him till he should reappear. In three minutes he was back again with another case. This he placed beside the first and again withdrew. Instantly Rawlins crept to the slip. The case was similar to that he had seen at Kaiseraugst. He tested its weight, then slipped silently back behind his shrub.

The Kaiseraugst operations were then repeated. Dolbey pulled up and made fast his boat, lifted the cases in, cast off and rowed to the *Komforta*. Again the skiff vanished against the launch's dark side, and again all sound and movement ceased. Again for something like two hours Rawlins watched, as before growing cold and cramped. Then shortly before three the boat reappeared and tied up at the slip.

ANYTHING TO DECLARE?

Dolbey lifted out his three cases and started off with the first.

Now came a modification of the previous plan. Instead of taking the case to the house, Dolbey carried it to his garage. He opened the door and lifted it inside. In a couple of minutes he emerged, obviously *en route* for the second.

Rawlins had intended during Dolbey's next absence again to try the case for weight. Now there wasn't time for that. It looked as if Dolbey were going to drive them away. Rawlins therefore crept from the shrub and hurried back to his car. He had parked it facing Ramsgate, believing that if Dolbey drove the stuff off, it would be in the direction of the larger town. Now he got in, started the engine, and sat waiting.

He was little more than in time. In a couple of minutes a car came out of Dolbey's drive and turned south towards Sandwich. Rawlins let it go a short distance, then turned his car and followed.

Presently they came to the outskirts of Sandwich. There was a certain amount of traffic on the road, mostly lorries, and lest he should lose his quarry in the town, Rawlins closed up. He was soon congratulating himself that he had done so. After crossing the Stour Dolbey turned right along the Canterbury road. Again Rawlins dropped behind. On deserted stretches of the road he went down to his side lights, as these wouldn't be seen by Dolbey and yet would keep him within the law.

They passed through Ash, Wingham and Littlebourne, and then about a mile from Canterbury Dolbey suddenly turned sharp left. Rawlins ran on past the place, which he saw was the gateway of a drive. Luckily there was a left-hand bend a little further on, and there out of sight of the gate he parked. Jumping out, he ran back.

PART 1: THE BITERS BITE

Cautiously passing in through the gates, he found himself in a well-sheltered drive. Between thick walls of laurel it rose steeply, turning quickly through almost a right angle. Just far enough from the gates to be screened from the road stood the car, its lights out. Dolbey had disappeared and Rawlins peeped in through the open rear door. Two cases were within. Obviously Dolbey had removed the other and would presently be back for the next. Rawlins sank into the laurels to watch.

He had not long to wait. In three or four minutes Dolbey appeared. He picked up a case, which now seemed to be really heavy, and with it set off back the way he had come.

As soon as he thought it safe, Rawlins followed. Dolbey had turned up off the drive into a narrow path leading away at right angles to the road. Rawlins crept after him.

As he pressed on he saw that the drive made a semicircle up to the house and then past it to the garage. The path ran direct to the garage, forming a chord to the curve. All the way it was screened by laurels. The garage door was open, and Rawlins had just time to sink behind a shrub when Dolbey emerged. Rawlins remained hidden and Dolbey shortly returned with the third case, left it also within, locked the garage and departed. Rawlins listened, but he did not hear the car start up. He concluded Dolbey had let it run back out of the drive by gravity.

It was now getting on towards four and Rawlins thought it unlikely that anything more would be done that night. He could scarcely get into an hotel, so he ran a mile out into the country, parked at the side of the road, and went to sleep in the car. About eight he woke, drove to a small hotel in Canterbury and shaved and breakfasted. Then he sat in the lounge ostensibly reading the papers while he considered his next step.

ANYTHING TO DECLARE?

So far, he thought, he had done extraordinarily well. He had proved that a nefarious trade was being carried on, and he had traced the passage of the smuggled objects from Switzerland to this house in the suburbs of Canterbury. The smugglers' scheme – if they were smugglers – seemed to him quite first class. He did not believe that anything could possibly be learnt about it except through some unlikely accident such as had happened in his own case. Now he had just to carry on a little longer and he would have these people where he wanted them. They would pay, he thought exultingly, and he wondered what terms he should demand. A lump sum: say, five thousand pounds? Or perhaps a thousand a year? His mouth, figuratively speaking, watered at the thought of it. All the same he had a lot more to learn before he could put on the screw. He must carry his researches further and the immediate question was, how was he to do it?

After some thought he believed he saw his way. While at the drive he had noted the name of the place: Mountjoy Cottage, Acacia Avenue. Now he went to the public library and looked up a directory. The occupant of Mountjoy Cottage was Bruce Baldwin.

He left the library and entered a telephone booth. There he looked up Baldwin in the telephone directory. There were several of the name and when he read one of them he felt he had reached his goal. It was: The Bruce Baldwin Watch Manufacturing Company, 210 Edison Street.

Rawlins could scarcely contain himself. So that was it! Duty-free Swiss watches! There could be no doubt whatever! Three boxes full every trip! Rawlins swore. Three boxes that size would mean a tidy sum. He needn't be niggardly in his claim.

PART 1: THE BITERS BITE

But he had yet to obtain actual proof that the Bruce Baldwin of Mountjoy Cottage and of the watch works were the same. Well, after what he had done, that would be child's play. He had a walk round and looked at the works, a small place in a slummy street. From such a works he imagined the boss would leave between five and six, and at quarter before five he parked far down the street. He soon found he had guessed well. At half past five the gates opened and a number of workers emerged. Then a pale green car of modern shape followed them and drove off in the opposite direction. Rawlins at once followed.

The chase led to a perfectly satisfactory conclusion. From far behind Rawlins at length saw the car turn into the Mountjoy Cottage drive. So that was that.

The essential part of the conspirators' scheme was now manifest, and once again Rawlins marvelled at its excellence. The loading up of the watches in Switzerland he had already seen to be foolproof save for some unlucky accident. The stowage on the launch must be quite first class, since neither he himself nor the Customs officers had been able to find any sign of them. And now the transport from launch to works had proved equally efficient. Dolbey never went to the works, nor did Baldwin approach the launch. Further, Dolbey and Baldwin never even met. Yes, it was certainly competent.

He could now understand why the unloading had not been carried out on the Saturday night. Baldwin could not deliver the watches to his works until Monday morning, and he naturally would not wish to have them in his garage over Sunday.

Rawlins then considered his own work. If the launch party's was good, his own was super. Not many people, he felt sure, could have done as well. And he had been strong-minded enough to keep the thing to himself. The payment that he would get from these men would therefore be all his own and undivided.

That brought him to the second part of his scheme: the obtaining of the money. He had thought out how to set about it. But first he must get away from Canterbury. There might be others in the thing besides Baldwin and Dolbey and he must not be seen by any of them. He therefore paid his bill at the hotel and returned to Ramsgate.

One further preliminary in this second part of his plan still required attention, but it was too late that night to deal with it. Accordingly early next morning he went out and walked through some of the narrower and shabbier streets of the town. Presently he saw what he was looking for, a small decayed looking stationer's. He entered, drew the ancient proprietor aside, and asked him could he furnish him with an accommodation address?

It appeared that the old man had never done such a thing, but half crowns were desirable, and for that sum for each letter handled he was willing to oblige. Rawlins then passed over a retainer in the shape of a ten shilling note and said that his name was Samuel Hunter. Any letter which came for him was to be kept till he called. Further, the arrangement between them was private and not the business of any other person.

This matter arranged, Rawlins returned to his hotel and began drafting a crucial letter. Though he knew what he wanted to say, he had some difficulty in putting it into suitable words. He wanted as far as possible to achieve a literary production, unlikely to have been composed by a mere male nurse. At last after many drafts he produced the following:

PART 1: THE BITERS BITE

Personal and Strictly Confidential.

Bruce Baldwin, Esq.,
The Bruce Baldwin
Watch Manufacturing Company,
210 Edison Street,
Canterbury.

20th August

Dear Sir,
I wish to approach you in a friendly rather than a defiant way and hope we may reach a conclusion in the same spirit.

This is to inform you that I have discovered the details of a certain scheme which starts with Mr Furnell and ends with your good self, passing intermediately through the hands of Messrs Loxton, Edgley and Dolbey; a scheme which reminds me of the old tag 'The Watch on the Rhine'. I congratulate you, sir, on having hit on so profitable an undertaking.

My knowledge, as you must see, has put me in a somewhat privileged position, and I am sure you will agree that I am entitled to share in the profits. I thought a single lump sum of five thousand pounds (£5,000) would meet the case, or if you prefer, an annual amount of one thousand pounds (£1,000) for seven years, either payment to complete all transactions between us.

The payment to be in Treasury notes, to be packed in a suitcase and deposited in the Cloak Room at the departure side of Waterloo Station. The ticket to be sent to me at the following address: c/o Alex Coote, 24 The Fairway, Ramsgate.

Perhaps I may add that attempted action against me personally would be ill-advised, as I have protected myself. I have sealed in an envelope a full account of your affair and handed it to my bank manager. I have told him that I will call to see him once each week, and asked him to send the envelope to Scotland Yard should I in any week fail to do so.

Trusting, as I said, to have an amicable reply,
I am, sir,
>   Yours faithfully,
>   SAMUEL HUNTER.

Rawlins had bought some cheap writing paper and envelopes. On this he copied his letter, addressed it to Baldwin at his works marking it "Personal and Confidential", and then went out and posted it. He realized that the paper might bear his fingerprints, but he thought this immaterial. He believed that even if Baldwin discovered his identity, his mythical letter to the bank manager would keep him safe. For a moment he toyed with the idea of writing such a letter to a bank, then he rejected the idea. If through some mischance he was prevented in any week from calling, he would have given himself away. Scotland Yard would act as ruthlessly against him as against the launch party.

Excited and a little nervous, he braced himself to wait for Baldwin's reply.

– 7 –

THE COUNTER BLAST

At his usual hour on the morning after Rawlins posted his letter, the Wednesday of that fateful week, Bruce Baldwin arrived at his works. He drove his car in through the big gates, then having unlocked the new garage he had recently had built, he placed the car therein, relocked the doors, and crossed the yard to his office.

The building of the garage had been a source of some adverse comment among his small staff. At the end of the yard there was an overhanging roof beneath which the firm's two small vans stood when out of use, and for years the space beside them had been good enough for the boss' car. It was true that the roof was not a complete protection on windy days, though normally sufficient. But Baldwin had suddenly become dissatisfied with it, and money which could have been better spent in increasing his staff's wages was poured out on this elaborate brick structure with its strong steel-bound doors. What the staff did not realize was that the wall against which the building had been placed contained a small door leading into the stores. Nor were they aware that every five weeks since it had been built, Edwin Campion, the storekeeper, had carried in through it hundreds of excellent Swiss watches which were afterwards sold for the benefit of himself, his chief, and the others who had assisted in their acquisition.

As Baldwin reached his office he could not help feeling a glow of warm satisfaction. This Swiss scheme was really doing extraordinarily well. The launch had now made four trips and each had been wholly successful. On the previous evening Campion had told him that two thousand more watches of excellent quality had been in the cases left in his garage by Dolbey and which he had on the Monday morning driven to the works. There was moreover nothing to suggest that the supply should ever dry up. Of course he knew that eventually it must do so, but that would be in the distant future. So far there had not been a hitch nor the slightest suggestion of suspicion. Already the outlay on the scheme had been recouped, and from now on every trip should show a clear profit.

It was not only the easy money which appealed to Baldwin. He gloried in the scheme also because it was his own child. He had met Loxton and heard of the *Komforta* and suddenly the idea had occurred to him. It had taken time and trouble to develop the plan, but eventually he had solved every problem and worked out every detail. Its success was therefore the more gratifying. He remembered with amusement his hesitation in approaching Campion, and his surprise and pleasure at the eagerness with which the storekeeper had leaped at the proposal. The others also had seemed delighted at the chance to join in, and he had to admit that each and every one of them had fully pulled his weight.

It was perhaps this very mood of optimism that produced a sudden reaction of feeling when he saw on the pile of his opened letters one in a not too well formed hand marked "Personal and Confidential". Instinctively he felt it

PART 1: THE BITERS BITE

presaged evil. If it did, he mustn't show any signs of preoccupation or distress before his sharp-eyed secretary. He therefore thrust the letter into his pocket, and having rung for Miss Emerson, went on with the remaining correspondence. He was satisfied that his manner while dictating replies and giving instructions was entirely normal, as it was also when he performed his next routine duty, an inspection of the work in hand. Returning to his office, he rang for certain books which would keep him busy for an hour or two. It was not till Miss Emerson had departed that he drew the letter from his pocket.

When he had mastered Rawlins' effusion he felt a strange and unpleasant sinking of his heart. The letter was a shattering blow. It was not so much that someone had tumbled to what they were doing, though that was bad enough in all conscience. If only one person was concerned, he could no doubt be dealt with. But what appalled Baldwin was the general breakdown in their scheme, that all their carefully thought out precautions had failed to preserve their secret. How had the leakage occurred? What part of the plan had broken down? If this Samuel Hunter had learnt the truth, what was to prevent others – including the Government officers – from doing the same? For a time Baldwin was too much aghast to think consecutively.

His first clear conclusion was that the affair was too important to be handled by himself alone. It was a matter for all of them. If drastic action had to be taken, the responsibility must be shared.

When once more he felt himself under control he rang for Miss Emerson. "I had an offer for some spring steel yesterday: met Mr Randall in the street. I'd like to talk to

Mr Campion about it. You might ask him to come over when he's free."

In a few minutes the storekeeper appeared and Baldwin did discuss the steel with him. Then because Miss Emerson's ears were as keen as her eyes he wrote on a memo: "Serious trouble. Will pick you up at corner of Castle Street at 1.15", and laying his finger on his lips, held it up before Campion. When the latter had read it and nodded he burnt it, covering the smell with a cigarette each.

At lunch time Baldwin got out his car, saying to Miss Emerson that he had forgotten some papers and would run home for them after lunch. Campion was waiting for him at the rendezvous and they drove out into the country. There Baldwin produced the letter.

If Baldwin had been dismayed by it, Campion was infuriated. That anyone should steal their secret and threaten their profits made him see red. Vengeance was his only idea: to wipe this intruder off the face of the earth.

Baldwin let him blow off steam, then sharply told him to pull himself together and talk sense. But when he found that the storekeeper's ideas did really run to murder, he listened more carefully.

"I confess murder had occurred to me too," he presently admitted, "but only as an ultimate possibility. I think and believe we can manage without it. But because it is a possibility I thought we should have a general meeting to consider the situation. The responsibility for whatever we do must be shared."

Campion slapped his knee. "You're wrong, Baldwin," he declared decisively. "If there's going to be anything serious, "we'll keep it to ourselves. What do you think we'd gain by consulting the others?"

PART 1: THE BITERS BITE

"Why should we do their dirty work for them?"

"That's nonsense and you know it. If we were caught, nothing could save us. It wouldn't help us if the others were in the soup too."

"They should take their share and run the same risks."

"That's just silly. Our fate, not theirs, is what matters to us. Besides, Baldwin, if it was murder they wouldn't come in. Dolbey might, but neither Loxton nor Edgley would have anything to do with it. They mustn't know: not anything. Not even about the letter."

"You think so?" Baldwin sounded troubled.

"Of course I think so. And what's more, it would be better if Dolbey wasn't told either. The fewer people who know about a thing, the less likely it is to come out. You and I are safe. Let's keep the thing in our own hands."

Baldwin made a gesture of assent. "Very well, I agree, at least in the meantime. The question then arises, what do we do?"

Campion swore. "We kill the blighter: that's what we do."

"And the letter at his bank?"

Campion moved uneasily. "We'd have to get hold of that," he said. "But I don't know how we'd do it."

"Nor I at the moment. But I suppose we could work out something. If we got him into our power I dare say we could make him write for it or telephone or both. I can even imagine that we could scare him into going for it."

"I suppose there is a letter?"

"Ah, now you're talking. I've been thinking over that and I doubt it very much. You see, it's a double-edged weapon. Suppose for some reason Hunter doesn't pay his weekly call at the bank. Suppose he meets with an accident: is knocked down in the street and taken, we'll say, to hospital. What happens then? The letter is sent to the police and it immediately convicts Hunter of blackmail and of being an accessory after the fact in the running of the watches. I doubt he'd risk such a letter."

"He mightn't have thought of all that."

"He must be pretty wide awake to have found out what he has. I don't think he'd miss the implications of the letter. But our trouble is that we don't know for sure, and we can't run risks."

"Then what's your own view?" As always Campion, after forcefully demanding strong action, drew back and turned to Baldwin for a lead.

"Well," Baldwin answered slowly, "as a matter of fact I've thought of a scheme that I believe could put Hunter out with absolute safety to ourselves. But we'll leave that for the present. Before we can consider it we must deal with two points. First, to find out if Hunter is playing a lone hand or if others are also in the thing and second, to get hold of the bank letter or make sure there isn't one."

"Neither easy."

"Neither easy, as you say. But our first step is easy, indeed quite obvious. That is to find out who Hunter is. We should get that through the address he gives. Find out who lives there, and if it's not Hunter himself, watch for him calling."

"Ah yes, that's something to be getting on with. If you put me down in Market Street I can run down to Ramsgate and see what the place is like."

"Good idea. I'll do so."

"There's another thing, Baldwin. I wanted to keep this to ourselves, but if the place is to be watched, neither you nor I can do it. We couldn't leave the works without starting talk."

"Dolbey?"

PART 1: THE BITERS BITE

"That's what I think. He's a stranger and he's free in the daytime. He can tell Loxton some yarn about a relative's illness. Can you get hold of him?"

"Yes, I'll see to that. You reconnoitre The Fairway and come up before five and we'll go into it further."

When Baldwin had dropped the storekeeper he pulled up at a telephone kiosk and rang Dolbey. Having made sure that the man was alone, he went on: "There's rather serious trouble and I must see you at once. Run out to the Grange Cross Roads at five forty-five today, park and walk towards Whitstable. I'll pick you up."

Reaching his office, Baldwin again sent for books which would normally keep him occupied. But he did no more than open them. Drawing a sheet of paper towards him, he began drafting a letter. It gave him a lot of trouble and practically every sentence was altered and rewritten many times before it satisfied him. It finally read:

PERSONAL.
Mr Samuel Hunter,
c/o Mr Alex Coote,
24 The Fairway, Ramsgate.

21st August

DEAR SIR,
I have your letter of 20th inst. and do not pretend that it is not somewhat of a shock. I have gone into the matter carefully with such of my colleagues as were available, and we are agreed that your position is strong and that we shall have to do something to meet your views.

First, as to the lump sum. The amount you mentioned is, as you might have known, quite absurd.

Up to the present our profits have gone in repaying the loans we obtained to set up our business, and this is only now beginning to pay. We have not the sum you mention among us all.

The annual contribution suggested as an alternative is also unsatisfactory to us, as it would leave us with no security and no guarantee against further demands.

At the same time we are agreed that your reasonable claim should be met. Your letter and recent achievement have proved your exceptional ability and we therefore make you this offer: We require another helper to oversee distribution in this country, and we offer the job to you on equal terms with ourselves. We cannot say exactly what this would bring you in, but we estimate about £1,500 a year. This would give you more money than you asked for and it would give us the security we desire.

I need scarcely point out to so knowledgeable a person as yourself, that if you bring our enterprise to an end, you will get nothing at all.

I shall be glad to hear from you at your convenience.
    Yours faithfully,

        BRUCE BALDWIN.

He had not much more than completed this effusion when he heard Campion's voice in the outer office: "Boss engaged?" and Miss Emerson's reply: "I don't think so, Mr Campion. I'll see." A knock followed and soon Campion was seated at the other side of his principal's desk.

"Got those specifications," he said loudly for Miss Emerson's benefit. "I wish you'd run your eye over them."

"Right, let's have them."

PART 1: THE BITERS BITE

Campion leant forward and spoke in a whisper. "That address is a small tobacconist's and stationer's. Hunter must be using it as an accommodation address."

"I thought that not unlikely," Baldwin replied in the same way. "It's a poor part of the town for all its name. Now we must have it watched. I'm meeting Dolbey in an hour to fix it up. In the meantime read that draft," and he handed over his letter. Campion read it with obvious approval.

"It's fine," he declared, still in a low voice. "It's the best way out. I don't know how you think of these things, Baldwin. But will the others stand for losing so much of their profits?"

"If you can suggest anything else, I'd be glad to hear it."

"I can't; I couldn't have suggested this. But it seems a pity to lose a seventh of the profits."

"Man alive," Baldwin said testily, "what are you thinking about? We'll not lose it."

"Not lose it? How do you mean?"

"Why, obviously after we get him in there'll be an accident."

Campion smiled grimly. "As I said before on different occasions, I'll hand it to you, Baldwin. Right. It's a good proposition and I'll not fail in my bit."

The talk on the specification Campion had brought in was resumed in more normal tones and presently the storekeeper withdrew.

The works closed at five-thirty and Baldwin, as was his custom, left at the same time. He drove off in the direction of his home, then turned towards the Grange Cross Roads. He saw Dolbey's car parked nearby and on the Whitstable road presently overtook the man himself. Having picked him up, he handed him Hunter's letter. "Read that," he said as they drove on.

ANYTHING TO DECLARE?

Dolbey was much more upset by the leakage than had been Campion. "It's just a calamity," he declared. "If this fella Hunter could find out what we're up to, sure couldn't the Customs people do the same? Have you told the others?"

"Campion, yes. He thinks with you, as of course I do myself. Loxton and Edgley, no. And they mustn't be told. They mustn't suspect even. This is important, Dolbey, and I count on you to keep it quiet."

"To be sure I will. But if it's important isn't that a reason for consultation among us all? What's the difficulty about it?"

"Just that if we have to take any drastic step – I hope and believe we won't have to – but if we do those two wouldn't stand for it. Conscientious scruples, if you like. Anyhow, we couldn't risk telling them."

Dolbey whistled. "So that's the idea, is it? Well, you won't find any conscientious scruples with me. I'd put a knife between the fella's ribs as soon as wink, if I got the chance."

"I don't think it'll come to that, but one must be prepared for everything. Now, Dolbey, I've thought out a scheme for dealing with the situation, and Campion agrees to it. We want your help."

"Sure you know you don't need to ask me that."

"I thought you'd feel that way. Now read this other letter," and he handed him his draft to Hunter.

Dolbey did so slowly and carefully, then shook his head. "It's a grand letter, Baldwin, brainy and puts the fella in a cleft stick and all that. But I don't see him getting a seventh of my share."

"That's what Campion felt and again of course I agree. But as I asked him, why should we pay anything? Suppose

PART 1: THE BITERS BITE

when we've learnt all about him and made sure no one else is in the know, he should meet with an accident?"

Dolbey favoured the other with a slow understanding look. "Ah," he said in satisfied tones, "that's the sort of talk. I'm with you, Baldwin, all the way. And I see now what you mean about Loxton and Edgley. You're right, they wouldn't stand for an accident. Now is there anything I can be doing at the present time?"

"Yes, Dolbey, there is. I type my letter and post it tonight and it's delivered in the morning. I want you to watch Coote's shop and see if you can spot Hunter when he calls for it. Then follow him and find out where he goes and anything else you can about him."

Dolbey drew a long breath. "Me the ruddy detective! Well, I can only do my best and I'll do that. It's a new job for me altogether."

"You'll manage all right. Now I must get back. I'll drop you near the crossroads and you carry on."

At his home Baldwin typed his letter, and running into Canterbury again after supper, posted it in a pillar-box near his office.

To say that Dolbey was appalled by Baldwin's news was putting it mildly. It was as if the entire bottom had fallen out of his world. The thing was just incredible. Their scheme was so good and it was carried out so well that no one, *no one*, could possibly have tumbled to it. That had been his conviction, and now in spite of this astounding revelation of Baldwin's, his belief was only shaken. Surely, he thought, there must be some mistake? And yet Hunter's letter did not leave much room for doubt.

Though puzzled, Dolbey was practical and efficient in anything he undertook. He wasted little time in conjectures, but passed on to consider how best he could carry out his commission.

Naturally the first thing was to reconnoitre the ground. He packed a bag in case he should have to stay overnight, drove to Ramsgate, parked, and walked to The Fairway. It had been a good street in its day, and along one side were some fine old Georgian houses. Now they were shabby and neglected looking. Their walls were blotchy, their steps hollow, and the colours of their various paints of a uniform drabness. In front of the dingy curtains in many of their lower windows were notices of "Apartments", "Bed and Breakfast", and occasionally "Vacancies". These notices gave Dolbey an idea.

First he located Coote's shop. It was small and from the look of the window he imagined that within it was both dark and dirty. He glanced up and down the street. He could see no cover from which to observe the place, and much against his will he turned to the old houses across the road. One nearly opposite Coote's bore the two notices "Apartments" and "Vacancies". He pressed the bell.

Unhappily the "Vacancies" were all to the rear. He tried another house without success, but in his third attempt lay the charm. A little further down the street, but still well in sight of Coote's shop, a first floor front bed-sitting-room was available. The window was entirely satisfactory.

"This would do me the very best," he said to the elderly tired-looking landlady. Then lest he should arouse her suspicions he went on: "Now for the tug of war. What about terms?"

These were moderate and he agreed to them at once. "My luggage is at the station," he went on, "but anyway I think I should pay a week in advance and perhaps," he smiled at her, "you think the same. But there's maybe a

PART 1: THE BITERS BITE

snag. I'd be wanting to come in tonight, say, in an hour. Would you be able for that?"

The landlady, obviously delighted to let her room to such a tenant, said she could easily be ready. Dolbey therefore paid for his week, and saying he would return later, took his leave.

So far he had had incredible luck. It was just a chance that there had been lodging-houses in the street and little short of a miracle that a suitable room should have been vacant. He could just hope that his luck would stand.

He walked about for an hour, then having collected his bag from the car, returned to his new abode. His room was a fine one, lofty and well proportioned, with large windows, elaborate cornice mouldings, a rose centre on the ceiling and what Dolbey thought must be a valuable chimney piece. But all was in a sad state of repair, with its faded wallpaper and stained paint. The furniture was poor, the carpet threadbare and the washing arrangements primitive. But everything was spotlessly clean, and when Dolbey got into bed he found it unexpectedly comfortable.

Next morning he was early at his window and presently saw the postman coming round. He put at least one letter into Coote's door as he passed. Baldwin's reply to Hunter, thought Dolbey, was now in that box across the road.

In due course the landlady brought him breakfast. She was not talkative, for which he was thankful, and went off again as soon as she could. Dolbey moved his table to the window and kept up his watch while he ate.

It was perhaps an hour later that he saw a figure approaching which seemed vaguely familiar. As the man came nearer he stared till his eyes felt like popping out of his head. It was Rawlins, his uncle's attendant. What could

Rawlins be doing in Ramsgate at nine-thirty in the morning?

Then his astonishment grew. With a suggestive little glance behind him the attendant turned into Coote's. Two minutes later he emerged and went on down the street in the same direction as before.

Dolbey was now overtaken by a sudden spasm of doubt. Should he shadow Rawlins or should he find out from Coote if he really had the letter? Baldwin had said to follow the man, but the circumstances were not those Baldwin had envisaged. Dolbey knew Rawlins and could doubtless put his hand on him at any moment. But he was not sure that Rawlins was his man. If while he was trailing Rawlins the real Hunter collected his letter, he would have let his partners down badly. He left the house and walked along the street, then crossing, returned and entered the shop. Holding himself with military stiffness, he spoke in a sharp though polite tone: "Good morning. Mr Alex Coote?"

The proprietor was elderly and stooped and like the landlady looked as if the burden of life was heavy. The shop was as dark, untidy and dirty as Dolbey had expected.

"My name, sir," said Coote flatly. "What can I do for you?"

"Sergeant John Willoughby, Criminal Investigation Department, New Scotland Yard," Dolbey declared crisply. "I want a small item of information from you."

Coote exhibited signs of anxiety. "I hope, sergeant, there's nothing wrong? I'm not conscious of – "

"Nothing whatever, so far as you're concerned, Mr Coote. It's entirely about a customer of yours. You have only to answer my question and you'll hear no more of the matter."

"And what's the question, sir?"

PART 1: THE BITERS BITE

"The man who left your shop five minutes ago. Did he get a letter addressed to Mr Samuel Hunter?"

Coote hesitated. "Well you know, sir, I undertake that such dealings with me will be confidential. I don't – "

"Now, Mr Coote, I'll ask you to think again about that." Dolbey's voice was sharper. "This man Hunter is suspected of a serious crime, and if you try to shield him you may find yourself charged as accessory after the fact. Give your information and you've nothing more to fear."

This was clearly a new idea to Coote and Dolbey could see that it was having its effect. All the same the old man was obviously unwilling to break faith with his customer. He did not appear to question Dolbey's bona fides, though Dolbey was prepared for a demand to see his card. He would have said that he had inadvertently left it in his uniform, agreed that until he showed it Coote was not bound to answer him, but at the same time would have threatened him severely enough to break his resistance.

But Coote did not raise the point. He struggled ineffectively to avoid an answer, then gave way. His caller was Mr Samuel Hunter. Dolbey thanked him, repeated that the matter would not be raised again, and left. He thought that he had himself probably broken the law by masquerading as a policeman, but as no one was ever likely to know of it, he was not unduly worried.

He walked briskly away from the shop considering what his next step must be. Should he ring up Baldwin and tell him what he had learnt? No, he thought, for he had not yet learnt enough. Until he found out where Rawlins was and how to get in touch with him, Baldwin could do nothing more. It would be foolish to run the risk of telephoning merely to satisfy Baldwin's curiosity.

ANYTHING TO DECLARE?

How could he find out where Rawlins was? Well, there was one way. The Gables! If he ran over to Folkestone and called on his uncle he could doubtless learn all he wanted. There was no reason why he should not do this at once. He went to the garage, got his car, and drove off.

The discovery that their blackmailer was Rawlins had come to Dolbey as a profound relief. A known enemy was less dangerous than one who struck from the dark. But that was not his chief reason. Rawlins, he remembered, had been with his uncle's party on the expedition to Switzerland. Obviously it must have been during the cruise that he had tumbled to what was going on. Therefore in all probability Rawlins was acting alone. Certainly no other member of the party could be his confederate, and it was unlikely that the attendant had shared his knowledge after his return, as this would have meant sharing the swag.

Some hour and a half later he reached Folkestone. He must offer his uncle some reason for his visit, and with this in view he called on his old chief in the engineering firm. He did not want to see the gentleman, but he thought it not unreasonable that in memory of old times he should look in to pass the time of day. He was well known in the town and his uncle might easily hear that he had been there.

It was getting on to midday when he arrived at The Gables. On this lovely morning Dr Marsham and Nancy were working in the garden. Both hailed him as if they were really glad to see him and Dolbey had the grace to feel slightly ashamed. In due course the doctor asked him what had brought him to the neighbourhood.

"Just a technical matter in my old office," Dolbey answered. "I'd had the handling of it and they wanted to know what I'd done. For the sake of an hour's drive I

PART 1: THE BITERS BITE

thought I'd come over and explain. Easier than writing it all down, you know."

"Well, we're very glad to see you at all events," Marsham answered. "You'll stay to lunch of course?"

Dolbey thanked him and agreed. They chatted and he had a walk round the garden and admired the flowers. He noticed that Nancy and Edith between them helped the doctor about and that Edith waited at table. It was therefore natural and unsuspicious that he should ask about Rawlins.

"On holidays," Marsham explained. "He asked for this week and of course he was entitled to it and got it."

"Sure can't we all do with a holiday," Dolbey rejoined. "Then he's coming back?"

"Yes. He's really due on Saturday midday, but I told him he needn't show up till the late evening."

"He's a good chap, Rawlins," Dolbey said carelessly. "Personally I never cared much for him, but he's the very man for you."

"He suits me admirably," Dr Marsham replied and the subject dropped.

After lunch Dolbey drove to Dover and from a call box rang up the Baldwin Works. Though no one in the office had heard him speak, he simulated a Scots accent in talking to the woman who answered him, only resuming his own voice when he heard Baldwin's. "I'd like a word with you," he said. "Where can we meet?"

"Same place and time as yesterday," Baldwin returned and rang off.

At a few minutes after half past five Dolbey parked, again near the Grange Cross Roads, but in a different place to that of the previous day. He walked as before towards Whitstable and as before Baldwin picked him up. The watchmaker seemed nervous and shaken. "Well," he breathed as soon as they were under way, "how have things gone?"

"Not too badly," Dolbey rejoined. "I think I've got what we want," and he recounted his adventures.

Baldwin was obviously impressed. "Good work, good work!" he declared. "I said you could do it. But that's an extraordinary coincidence that you should know the man! It's a bit of luck we couldn't have counted on."

"Ah, not so extraordinary as all that," Dolbey returned. "Sure wasn't it through me the fella went on the trip? My uncle came down to look at the tide turbine and saw the *Komforta* and it all arose out of that."

"Yes, yes, I know. But I think it was a coincidence all the same and very lucky for us."

"Well, we've got the information anyway. Maybe I should have followed him to find out where he was staying, but I thought the other more important."

"What you did was better. If you'd followed him he might have seen you. Now, as you say, we have the information and he doesn't know it. But I don't understand how he got on to the thing. He must have seen something on the *Komforta*."

"Must have done, I suppose. But there's one good thing about it," and Dolbey gave his reasons for believing that Rawlins was playing a lone hand. Baldwin was clearly still more impressed. He thought it over and said he was sure Dolbey was right. "Well, we can leave explanations till later on," he continued. "Now as to what we're to do next. I suppose wait for the man's reply to my letter?"

Dolbey moved uneasily. "I've been thinking about that, Baldwin, indeed I might say I've thought of nothing else

PART 1: THE BITERS BITE

this entire day, and I've got a suggestion. I believe maybe it would do what we want."

"Go ahead. Grateful for anything."

Dolbey instinctively leant forward and lowered his voice. He spoke for some moments while Baldwin at intervals nodded and grunted. Then for a time there was silence broken only by the murmur of the smooth running engine and the purring of the tyres. At last Baldwin seemed to make up his mind.

"I declare, Dolbey, I believe you've got it. Let me go over that again. We keep Rawlins busy with negotiations till Saturday. On Saturday afternoon Loxton and Edgley start on their next trip. That leaves you and Campion and me with a clear field and on Saturday evening we settle the thing. Yes, I believe that'll do it. Fine work, old man! Now there's a snag. We can get over it of course, but it needs thinking about."

"What's that?"

"There's quite a lot to be done to get things ready and this is Thursday evening. We've got less than forty-eight hours."

Dolbey considered this. "Ah, that's no snag at all. Sure can't we divide the thing up between the three of us?"

"I think we'll have to. How would this do? You're the mechanic, you produce the number-plates. I'm an office man, I do the letter. Campion's an authority on boats, he buys the outboard motor and chain."

"That'll do the very best. But Campion ought to go, say, to Margate for the motor, for that's a bit further from the Stour. Also he should go first thing in the morning. If he can't get the right thing he may have to try elsewhere."

"I'll give him a hint about it. I suppose he knows the size of your boat?"

"Well you thought of that. He may not." Dolbey scribbled in his notebook, then tore out the page. "There's a sketch with dimensions. That'll be all he'll want."

"Good. I'll see him tonight. Tomorrow he can have leave of absence to visit a relative who has met with an accident."

"He can so."

"On second thoughts I don't think it would be wise for any one of us to make two purchases. If some nosy policeman found it out he might get ideas. Campion can deal with the motor, but I'll buy the chain."

Dolbey agreed, but neither man realized the momentous issues which were to stem from this apparently trivial decision.

– 8 –

THE SETTLEMENT

When Baldwin had gone Dolbey walked slowly back to his car. As his scheme required a few other purchases and Ramsgate seemed as good a place as any to make them in, he decided to spend another night in his room. His landlady looked at him anxiously when he told her that a friend had asked him to stay at his house and he would therefore be leaving in the morning. But when she found he was not going to claim a refund on his week's rent she resumed her normal air of pessimistic endurance.

Next morning he made his purchases, a quantity of the plastic of which children make models and tins of white and black Chinese lacquer. Also for his subsequent disguise a pair of clear glass tortoiseshell spectacles "for amateur theatricals" and the cap and clothes of a labourer. He drove all to his workshop, where he hid them behind other stores. Then he went to the river and hailed Loxton to explain his absence. Loxton was politely concerned to learn that Dolbey's sister had met with an accident and he hoped it would not prove so serious as had at first been feared.

"I'm off to London presently," he went on. "Some question of insurance has arisen and I think I'd better see the people. I'll stay overnight and meet some other friends."

This was highly satisfactory to Dolbey. He wanted a few undisturbed hours in his workshop, and though Loxton seldom looked in, he did so occasionally. But for some reason Edgley never entered the place, calling at the cottage if he wanted anything.

When Loxton had gone Dolbey started work. From some sheet metal which he used for his turbine he cut pieces the size of Baldwin's number-plates, turning down a fold all round to give the necessary strength. On each he fixed a piece of oak, shaped to engage with the brackets on the car. Then came the letters. These he laboriously formed from plastic, giving the strokes a triangular cross section. To make it easier he chose letters and numbers without curves. Then he pressed his creations on to screws put through the plate from the back, and the construction was complete. It was a slow job and lasted till the evening.

Next day, the Friday, the plastic having set hard, he coloured his masterpiece with the lacquers in the approved black and white. Though not a permanent job, it was excellent for temporary use.

But even then it was not quite finished. Dolbey returned to his house and there swept such carpets as it contained. In spite of the ministrations of his daily help, he obtained a considerable quantity of dust. Before his last coat of lacquer was completely dry he showered this thinly on the plates. The result, as seen from a little distance, was that the new plates became old.

That night he secretly drove to Baldwin's and left his masterpiece in the garage. In the garage also was the chain which Baldwin had bought and this he transferred to his own car. He then went on to Campion's and collected the outboard motor, which the latter had earlier left in an outhouse.

PART 1: THE BITERS BITE

Though these jobs had to be done, Dolbey had plenty of time to think and in spite of the fact that it was only one day till their great adventure, time began to drag interminably. Having no one to talk to about the affair produced a cumulative strain, and pretending to Loxton and Edgley that nothing was afoot, made this still more irksome.

Early on that Saturday morning there was a message from Baldwin. "Pick you up at your drive at four this afternoon."

Dolbey gave a sigh of relief. All must be going well. Four o'clock was zero hour according to his plan. The *Komforta* left for Ramsgate about three, and that would just give him time to get ready for the night.

Though this was good as far as it went, the intermediate hours dragged more slowly than ever. Anxiety and fear remained gnawing at his mind. His was the plan, and though Baldwin and presumably Campion also had approved it, he felt that his was still the major responsibility.

But in spite of his uneasiness, everything during the day went normally. The *Komforta* "crew" completed their preparations to time and just at three she sailed. By the time she had passed out of sight round the bend of the river Dolbey had the outboard motor in his boat and was ready to test it. A further great relief surged up in his mind when it started up at once and ran strongly and in reasonable silence. He put it away in his garage and made sure the door was securely locked.

One small matter remained, his disguise. He had prepared it in the way beloved of detective novelists, though whether adopted in real life he did not know. He put on the tortoiseshell spectacles and the workman's clothes, adding pads of rubber to swell out his cheeks. He assumed a lazy slouching walk which contrasted with his normal swinging gait. Baldwin and Campion were also to disguise themselves. Even the car was to be covered with dust instead of showing its usual gleaming polish, and Baldwin had undertaken to change the number plates as soon after leaving Canterbury as possible.

Having slipped a pair of binoculars into his pocket, Dolbey went out to the main road. In a few minutes a dirty uncared-for car appeared. It bore the registration number he had so painfully provided. Two strange men sat within, and Dolbey had to look twice before he saw that they were his associates.

"My word, you've done it the very best," he exclaimed as he got in. "Sure wasn't I wondering who was in the car. That's the way to succeed."

"We'll succeed all right," Baldwin returned grimly. "The *Komforta* gone?"

"Left at three as usual. All well and no suspicions at all."

"Good."

"What about Rawlins?" Dolbey went on. "Any word from him?"

Baldwin felt in his pocket as he drove. He handed over a folded paper. It was a letter on the same block sheet and in the same handwriting as the first and bore the same title. It read:

22nd August

DEAR SIR,
I have yours of yesterday and note contents.

I thank you for the offer of a place in your scheme, but you will scarcely blame me if I decline to make myself liable in that way to a prison sentence. My terms remain as before, either £5,000 down or £1,000

PART 1: THE BITERS BITE

a year for seven years. I gather from what you say that the first alternative would be inconvenient to you, but cannot accept your suggestion that you could not at the present time fall in with the second. I would again ask you to put the required sum (£1,000) in Treasury notes in a suitcase, deposit it where stated, and send the key to me at the address previously used.

Should I receive the ticket within a week from today and in due course find the money in the suitcase you will hear nothing further from me for one year. If not, I shall be able to make my own profit from the Revenue authorities.

I am, sir,
      Yours faithfully,
           SAMUEL HUNTER.

"Not what you might call a compromising spirit," Dolbey commented. "It shows we're doing the right thing."

"Yes, it justifies us," Baldwin admitted, while Campion declared firmly; "Nothing else for it."

They drove south, turning inland and using minor roads which bypassed Sandwich, Deal and Dover, and bore towards the sea again behind Folkestone. Directed by Dolbey they approached the suburbs and entered a quiet residential road screened on both sides by trees and leading to but few houses.

"That's The Gables," Dolbey pointed. "You'd better turn and park on that grass plot at the side of the road." The place was a hundred yards or more from The Gables and twice that distance from the main road.

"Now," Baldwin said shortly, "time for you to do your stuff, Dolbey."

Dolbey nodded. He left the car and passed in among the trees. The spinney was typical heath land, with thickets of young birch and an occasional pine rising from matted heather and bracken. Dolbey had explored it on many occasions and his knowledge now enabled him to approach The Gables from the rear unseen from road or houses. He worked round among the bushes to where he could overlook the windows of the kitchen, Rawlins' pantry and the servants' bedrooms, all of which were in the back return. Then lying down among the shrubs, he took out his binoculars and settled down to watch.

It was still and pleasantly warm. The hum of insects and the song of birds suggested the open countryside far removed from a thriving sea coast town. But Dolbey was too intent on his business to hear birds or appreciate rural peace. What he wanted was to find out whether Rawlins had returned to the house, and knowing if he had he would at this time be in one of these rooms, he kept his eyes on the windows.

He could see Janet moving about the kitchen. For some time no one else appeared, then in Rawlins' pantry he saw Edith. Watching her for some time through his glasses, he became satisfied that she was doing Rawlins' work. As there was no sign of Rawlins in any of the other rooms, he concluded that the man had not yet arrived. After waiting a little longer to confirm his opinion, he carefully withdrew from his lair and worked his way through the wood back to the car.

"Not turned up yet," he reported.

"Good," said Baldwin. "We counted on that. It's now getting on to six and he probably won't arrive before nine or ten. So much the better for us if it's dark. But we can't stay here for four hours. We'd be seen and remarked on."

PART 1: THE BITERS BITE

"Ah, we're right enough," Dolbey declared. "See that," he pointed to a path which disappeared into the woods. "It leads to the top of the hill where there's a view. It's a place where people go, picnics and so on. We've only to get out and hide in the wood and anyone who sees the car'll think we've gone up."

"That sounds all right. You said you could let us know when he's coming?"

Dolbey nodded. "You go on up the path a bit. I'll stay near the road and keep watch."

"Okay." Baldwin and Campion went far enough into the trees to be hidden from both road and path while Dolbey remained on the look-out below. On several occasions he joined them to avoid passers-by, always returning to continue his vigil.

Now once again time began to crawl. For all three the minutes dragged more and more slowly and in spite of their efforts, anxiety as to the success of their plan grew keener. Seven passed and then after an eternity, eight. As dusk fell they returned to the car, switched on the side lights, and drew out on to the road. Baldwin raised the bonnet and bent over it, while Campion moved to the rear, opened the boot, and pretended to be looking for something therein. Dolbey left them and went to the main road. So once again they waited interminably.

Just at nine a bus ground up from the town and stopped at the end of the road. Many other buses had done the same thing, but all three grew more wary and tense as they imagined that the time of Rawlins' arrival must now be near. Dolbey had been certain he would use the bus, as he had never known him to arrive otherwise.

Presently a leisurely step was heard approaching from the road. Dolbey had slipped behind a shrub and soon the man, now dimly seen in the light of the single road lamp, passed his hiding place. A moment later Dolbey's torch shone out: three short flashes. It was his signal. The man was Rawlins.

As he came opposite the car bonnet Baldwin straightened up. "Excuse me," he said, "but is there any place about here where I could telephone? The car has crocked up." He manoeuvred Rawlins so that his back was to the rear of the car.

"Why, yes," Rawlins began. "If you'll come along with me – "

His voice died down suddenly into a throaty gurgle as Campion, creeping up behind him, threw a light rope round his neck and pulled it tight. Baldwin immediately, and Dolbey after a few seconds, joined in to prevent the unhappy victim from struggling. Dolbey quickly ran through his pockets and relieved him of his keys. He was then lifted into the back of the car, Campion following him and continuing his deadly pressure. Baldwin slid into the driving seat and started up the engine. The car moved slowly off.

Now came the second part of Dolbey's "stuff", a much more difficult exploit than the first. In short, he had to obtain Rawlins' passport. Obviously the man had had one when on the Swiss excursion, and almost certainly he would have kept it and it would be in his room. Dolbey had never been in the room, but he knew where it was and had seen into it when passing along the passage.

At this hour, during the news, the family would normally be listening in the lounge. Edith would have finished her evening chores and would doubtless be sitting with Janet in the kitchen. No one would be in the back passage or upstairs.

PART 1: THE BITERS BITE

There was danger of discovery of course. Anyone might be about the house on some special business. But Dolbey thought that if discovered he could bluster his way through by reason of his relationship to the doctor. He could pretend he had intended to startle them all as a joke. If they didn't believe him it wouldn't matter. They wouldn't say so.

Having put on rubber gloves, he dived once more into the trees and retraced his steps to the house. This time it was much darker and he walked openly across the grass to the front door. He stooped and listened at the keyhole of the large old-fashioned lower lock. All was still. Cautiously he inserted his Yale key into the upper lock. He opened the door, entered, and gently closed it again. The silence remained unbroken. He tiptoed across the hall, passed through the service door to the return and crept up the back stairs. In another minute he was in Rawlins' room with the door locked behind him. Very carefully he switched on his torch.

The room was simply but comfortably furnished. Besides the bed, dressing-table, easy chair, basin with running water and built-in wardrobe, there was only a small writing-table with drawers. He tried the drawers. All were locked. He had expected something of the sort. It was for this reason that he had postponed his entry, which could have been made more safely during dinner, till he had obtained Rawlins' keys. Now he could do his business without leaving traces or risking the sounds of splitting wood. No one in fact would know that the room had been entered.

A short search gave him the two things that he had come for. In one of the drawers was the passport and with a grunt of satisfaction he slipped it into his pocket. His second object was to find out if Rawlins had a bank account. Here also the evidence was satisfactory. Not a single book, paper or letter suggested such a thing. This he thought convincing. A cheque-book Rawlins might have taken away with him, but if there was an account, some other record of it would certainly be there. If on the other hand there was no account, Rawlins' statement about the letter he had left with his manager was false. Baldwin had already put forward reasons for believing it to be a bluff and this research seemed to confirm that view.

With the exception of the removal of the passport Dolbey left everything as he found it. Now he had only to get away and his mission would be accomplished. Silently he unlocked and opened the door and stood listening.

All remained still without. In his mind's eye he seemed to see Janet and Edith in their easy chairs in the corner of the kitchen and the others grouped in the lounge. Now was his chance. A few seconds and he should be out of the house.

Noiselessly he closed the door and began creeping down the back stairs. But he had not got halfway when the lounge bell rang. He guessed what it meant. The doctor was going to bed and in the absence of Rawlins, Edith would help him to his room.

Dolbey went up the few steps required to take him round the turn on the stairs and out of sight of the passage Edith would use. In a moment he heard her pass. The creak of the door to the hall followed and then its soft bump as it swung shut after her.

His easiest way out would have been through the kitchen and back door, but that was almost certainly blocked by Janet. He must therefore go as he had come, by the hall. Also he must go soon, for if once the hall door was locked he could scarcely pass through it. He could unlock it of course, but he could not relock it behind him. This would give away that a secret visit had been paid, which in its turn

PART 1: THE BITERS BITE

might break down the suggestion they intended to make that Rawlins had voluntarily disappeared.

He hurried down the stairs and very slightly opened the baize door to the hall. Yes, he had been right. He could hear the doctor's shuffling step and the sharper tap of heels. Then came Julia's voice speaking to Edith. The doctor was crossing the hall to his room. All three, he knew, would go into the room. Then would be his chance. He could get safely out if only Nancy did not choose that moment to leave the lounge on some errand. But that he must risk.

Directly he heard the others enter the doctor's room he slipped silently through the door and tiptoed across the hall to the porch. At that moment the doctor's door opened again. Julia was coming out.

Dolbey had no time to escape. He flattened himself against the porch wall, where he was partly hidden by the inner door frame. For a moment it seemed touch and go. But the footsteps crossed the hall and went upstairs and he knew that the danger was past. He waited till Julia had reached the upper landing, then softly opened the door, slipped out, and closed it gently behind him.

Outside in the dark he walked openly down the drive to the road. He had now only to find the car. Baldwin had refused to await him lest some zealous constable or seeker for local information should approach closer than might be healthy, but he had undertaken to drive continuously round an agreed circuit. Having reached this circuit Dolbey was to switch on his torch if he saw cars approaching, and when Baldwin saw the light he would stop.

The plan worked perfectly. The fourth car halted and Dolbey got in beside Baldwin. At a moderate speed they drove off. In the rear sat Campion and covered by a rug on the floor beside him was a large shapeless object.

ANYTHING TO DECLARE?

The dreadful deed had been carried out more easily than they had anticipated. And how completely it altered their situation! There was now no fear that their lucrative activities would be brought to naught, nor would they have to pay large sums to preserve a precarious secrecy. What they had done was admittedly horrible, but all felt that they were not to blame. Rawlins had asked for it. The man could have remained in perfect safety, but since he had chosen to become a blackmailer he could not expect to escape retaliation. No, they were justified in what they had done. Moreover they were safe – or practically safe. So far no suspicion had been aroused and no clues left. They had only to carry on and the whole ghastly business would be over and done with.

Baldwin was driving slowly through by-roads. At all costs he must avoid any kind of incident which might attract the attention of the police. The one thing which would mean deadly danger would be an accident or even the exceeding of the speed limit. They wanted to reach Dolbey's, but not while people were about. One in the morning they thought would be the earliest safe hour. So Baldwin was in no hurry and drove by a roundabout and devious route.

He timed the journey well. It was ten minutes past one when they stopped before Dolbey's garage. It was a big garage with room for two cars, otherwise Dolbey would have removed his own before setting out.

They lifted out the body and Baldwin went through the pockets. Presently he gave a grunt of satisfaction. "Here's my letter and copies of his," he exclaimed. "That's excellent. That destroys all written evidence against us."

"So he didn't send them to his bank," said Campion.

"Doesn't that look as if he hadn't a bank to send them to?"

PART 1: THE BITERS BITE

"He hadn't. If he'd had an account Dolbey would have found a record."

"One other matter," Baldwin went on. "Lend a hand here a moment."

He put on rubber gloves, then took from his pocket an envelope, extracted a letter, and laid it flat on the table.

"You can read that later," he told them, "but now I want to get Rawlins' prints on it. Will you lift him so that I can hold the hand over the sheet."

Campion and Dolbey did so. They supported the body while Baldwin grasped the right arm. Then one by one he pressed down the thumb and fingers in various positions on the sheet.

"This is a letter from Rawlins to Marsham, accounting for his absence," he explained as he worked. "I copied the writing from his letters to me, and I've been careful that no prints of mine have got on it. It should prevent any inquiries being made, but if suspicion should arise, Rawlins' prints should guarantee it."

"Fine, Baldwin! You think of everything."

"Someone has to." Baldwin folded the letter and replaced it in the envelope. "Now, Dolbey, if you get the boat ready, we'll carry him down."

This was the next step in the disposal of the body and it was here that their recent purchases came in. While Baldwin and Campion rolled the heavy chain round the body and fastened it with wire, Dolbey got the outboard motor into his boat. Then all three carried the body down, put it aboard, stepped in themselves, and rowed silently off.

The night was excellent for their purpose. It was calm and fairly dark. While they could dimly see their direction, they felt sure that they would be scarcely visible from the banks. Naturally they showed no light. The tide also was with them. High water had been about an hour earlier and the current was running strongly out. Of course this would be against them when they were returning, but if necessary they could use the motor till they were above Dolbey's slip, then drift back to it on their oars.

When they had passed out of the narrow river into Pegwell Bay they put up their proper lights and started the motor.

"How far do you want to go?" Baldwin asked Campion, who was the recognized authority in things maritime.

"Well, below low water level of course, but also where there's no fishing, particularly trawling. We can't be absolutely sure of that, but I think we'd be fairly safe in a mile and a half."

Some twenty minutes later Campion gave the signal. While he continued at the helm, the other two lifted the weighted body and tipped it overboard. It sank like a stone. Of Rawlins nothing now remained but a memory and probably some personal effects at The Gables. All three heaved sighs of relief as Campion turned the boat's head back towards the Stour.

Little was said on the return journey. None of them felt like conversation. The remembrance of murder does not sit lightly on the conscience. Already they were beginning to feel its weight.

Before entering the narrow river Campion doused the light, then lifted out the motor and threw it into the fairway. That possible clue was gone. They took to the oars and after a long stiff pull reached Dolbey's slip. It was still early, just a little after three.

"Better come in and see the letter," said Baldwin when the boat was moored and all left as before.

PART 1: THE BITERS BITE

Having made sure that the window curtains were lightproof, they sat down in Dolbey's living-room. Baldwin again put on his rubber gloves, took the sheet from the envelope, and once more laid it on the table.

"I need scarcely say 'don't touch it'," he warned. "I've taken the greatest care with it. I've even torn off half a dozen sheets below it on the pad, lest any of the downstrokes should have marked through."

"Better to have burnt the pad surely?"

"No good in that. I had used several sheets and they were all about my study. I should perhaps have bought a new pad, but I didn't think of it till too late."

They leant forward and read the letter as it lay. It was in Rawlins' handwriting, as copied from his two letters, and seemed an excellent forgery. It read:

George Marsham, Esq, MD,
The Gables,
Folkestone.

SIR,
I hope you will not think that I have acted too badly when I tell you that I have been forced unexpectedly to leave your service. While in London I was approached by a rich gentleman from Brazil. He offered me a position far better than I could ever hope to get in this country, on condition that I would start with him at once, for he was leaving that night for the Continent. I wanted to work my week's notice to you, but I could not. It was either go with him or lose the job. I had intended to spend a couple of days in Dieppe, so had my passport and could agree. For the sake of a week I

felt sure you would not stand in my way. I should be grateful if you would let Edith have my things.

I wish to express my great regret at any inconvenience I may have caused you and to thank you for your very good treatment of me while with you.

Yours obediently,
JOSEPH RAWLINS.

"Couldn't be better!" Campion approved when he had finished it. "It puts us in the clear all right."

"I always said you were the boy, Baldwin," Dolbey declared. "Sure it's just grand!"

"I think it'll do the trick," Baldwin admitted. "Well, partners, everything has gone better than we could have hoped. We've saved our enterprise and our money, and we've not left a single clue."

The others agreed. Then Baldwin glanced at his watch. "Just on to four," he observed, "on Sunday morning by the way. Now, Campion, you and I'll run up to London and post this. We'll breakfast in town and return later. I suppose you told your people you had a dinner there last night?"

"Yes. I think they swallowed it all right."

"So did mine."

Five minutes later the car backed slowly out of Dolbey's garage and drove quietly off.

Baldwin and Campion met with no difficulties in carrying out their plan. They reached London and posted the letter in a pillar box near the Marble Arch, on the assumption that a rich gentleman from Brazil might be expected to stay somewhere near Park Lane. Breakfasting at Victoria, they were back at their homes by midday. They met no one they knew and were satisfied they had left no trace of their expedition.

PART 1: THE BITERS BITE

For the three partners the next few days were decades of anxiety and fear. They heard nothing about Rawlins' disappearance, nor was there any note of it in such papers as they could get hold of. This of course was what they had hoped for, and yet to their troubled minds the silence seemed dark and menacing. They could not be sure that inimical forces were not mustering under its cover, and a possible evening visit by large solemn men was never far from their thoughts. Then they breathed more freely. Baldwin noticed in a London paper an advertisement from Marsham for a new attendant. All must therefore be well. Had suspicion been aroused, some member of the family would certainly have written such exciting news to Dolbey.

Their belief that all was well was confirmed as without incident time continued to pass. Then some seventeen days after the *Komforta* had sailed, Baldwin found a letter among his mail marked "Personal and Strictly Confidential". As he remembered a previous letter with a similar inscription he shivered. But when during Miss Emerson's absence from the office he opened it he felt, strong as he was, that he was going to faint. Indeed only recourse to the bottle kept for bringing to the point indecisive customers enabled him to take in its message fully. Like its predecessor it was typed on the usual sheet torn from the usual cheap pad. It read:

Mr Bruce Baldwin,
The Bruce Baldwin Watch Manufactory,
Canterbury.

DEAR SIR,
This is to inform you that through a lucky fluke I have discovered what you chaps are up to with your motor launch and your trips to Switzerland. Also I have

learned what happened to the last man who made the same discovery. I mean a man whose third letter was w and sixth n – you can supply the rest. What's more, I can prove both of these things to the police and be safe myself, for I can say at any time that I had only just got to know the details that gave them away. As evidence that I know what I am talking about I give you the name Furnell.

I don't want trouble either for myself or you, so I am coming down on you easy. I want an equal share of the swag with your own members, paid when they get theirs. As long as this is done I will hold my tongue, but on the first payment that's missed I'll find my evidence. But I want to tell you that you needn't try what you did before, for I'm well protected.

If you agree to this write to Hugh Kent, c/o James Nolan, 16 Friar's Lane, Ramsgate. I'll reply telling you what to do about the money.

Sick both in body and mind, Baldwin forced himself to make arrangements with Campion and Dolbey for a secret meeting that evening.

PART 2

The Biters Bit

– 9 –

THE CALL TO FRENCH

We must now go back some seventeen days in our history to the night when Joseph Rawlins met his fate, and see how the occupiers of The Gables reacted to his disappearance.

When on that eventful night he did not turn up, all assumed he had missed a train or coach and gave the matter little thought. When Sunday passed and there was still no sign of him the general feeling was mild irritation. Only the housemaid, Edith Jones, was seriously perturbed. She remembered the hint he had given her that his holiday might be profitable, and her own reply that if the amount proved satisfactory their early engagement might be considered. In the face of this she did not believe he would deliberately ignore her. Since therefore he had sent no message it looked as if he had been unable to do so.

But when on Monday morning the letter came saying he was off to Brazil, the feelings of the household were once more in unison. All condemned him, the family with exasperation, Edith with concentrated venom. He must, as she put it to herself, have been trifling with her affections. She now told herself that she had never had a very high opinion of him. All the same, that he would have treated her in so scurvy a way she would not have believed.

ANYTHING TO DECLARE?

During the Monday she fumed and raged internally, but that night, lying awake, doubts began to creep into her mind. On the whole Rawlins had treated her well and she believed he was really fond of her. There must be something about the Brazilian engagement which he had kept back in writing to Dr Marsham. If he found it satisfactory he would probably ask her to go out and be married there. He might not have had time to write a second letter to her, but doubtless she would get one in a day or two.

Presently she began to wonder if there was any phrase in the letter which might indicate that he had had this in his mind. Well, it was easy to find out. Letter and envelope were both in the waste-paper basket, where Dr Marsham had thrown them in his disgust.

She got out of bed and with a torch went silently down to the study. She got the letter, and having learnt from detective stories that envelopes were also of value, she retrieved it too. Back in her room she began to study them.

At first the letter seemed simple and straightforward, but as she pondered over the phrases her doubts returned. Edith was well-educated and knew literary English when she saw it. This was an admirable letter: but was it not too good? Somehow she could not see Rawlins expressing himself so well. Would he have said "a position far better?" Surely "A far better position" would have been his line. So with "For the sake of a week I felt sure you would not stand in my way". He would almost certainly have written "I felt sure you would not stand in my way for the sake of a week". The whole composition was unlike him.

There was also, she thought, something strange about the appearance of the letter, though for some time she could not decide what it was. Then suddenly she saw. The writing was level and yet there were no lines on the paper.

PART 2: THE BITERS BIT

Now this was something that Rawlins could never achieve. Without guidance his lines invariably dropped towards the end. When she added all this to his failure to turn up she felt completely puzzled.

So impressed was she by her doubts that in the morning she mentioned them to Janet, the cook. "There's something queer about it," she insisted. "Rawlins is not much to boast about, but I don't believe he'd have done a dirty thing like that. And I don't believe he could have written the letter without help. I'd like to know what you think?"

This was fishing and it obtained the desired bite. Young Sergeant Trimble of the local police had not long before fallen badly for Janet. He was a frequent visitor to the kitchen and more than once had hinted that now that he had got his step up a marriage might shortly be arranged. Janet was obviously impressed, but she had not yet reached a decision and for the time being Trimble was as wax in her hands.

"We'll ask Jimmy," she said, reacting perfectly to the stimulus. "He'll be in tonight and it'll be something for him to talk about instead of sitting there like a stuck pig glowering at me."

"He hasn't always a lot to say," Edith agreed and then to avoid any suggestion of criticism added, "though compared to Rawlins he's a chatterbox."

All through the day Edith's misgivings grew more intense. She felt that she was the only person who suspected a disaster and she became increasingly anxious to share her responsibility. She therefore hailed Trimble's arrival with relief.

When the three of them were seated round the table with glasses of Dr Marsham's beer, Janet opened the subject. "Edith's got some bee in her bonnet about Rawlins," she began. "He didn't turn up on Saturday at the end of his leave and wrote that instead he was off to Brazil. She thinks the whole thing's a bit fishy. She'll tell you. Go ahead, Edith."

Thus encouraged, Edith went ahead. She gave the sergeant a creditably clear and concise account of the affair, producing the letter and envelope for his inspection. He listened carefully and seemed impressed.

"My word, Edith, you don't half put up a case," he declared. "You should read for the bar and you'd make a hit. Just let's have some of those details over again."

Edith was secretly delighted when he drew a notebook from his pocket and began to jot down the salient points of her tale. Then he studied the letter.

"Got anything else with Rawlins' handwriting on it?" he asked presently.

"I can get you some letters from his room."

"Steady a mo. I'd like to have a look round the room."

"Why not? Come along with me."

This development was not so satisfactory to Janet and she raised the point that the sergeant should not be taken through the house till Dr Marsham had signified his approval. But Edith with insight answered, "You come along too," and the opposition was overcome.

Trimble began by getting the handwriting specimens. "I'll take these along with the letter," he explained, "and compare them later. Now I'd like a look round."

Nothing appeared to interest him till he came to the small writing table. Dolbey had had Rawlins' keys to open the locked drawers, but naturally he had relocked them before leaving. "I'd like to force these open," Trimble said. "Any objection, Edith? I suppose the table's yours."

PART 2: THE BITERS BIT

Edith shook her head. "Do anything you like," she told him, "if only you learn the truth."

Asking for a chisel, Trimble sprung up the division above drawer after drawer, releasing the bolts. He quickly ran through the contents, again without finding anything interesting.

"Something sharp here," he presently exclaimed, rubbing his finger. Then he stooped over the drawer. "Some little points pushed through the bottom from below."

He lifted the drawer out and turned it upside down. There, fixed to the under-side with drawing pins, was a Post Office Bank passbook. He disengaged and opened it.

"Bless my soul, Edith, you're in luck!" he exclaimed. "If all Rawlins' stuff is yours, there's over four hundred pounds for you in the bank!"

Both women at first were speechless, then Edith found her tongue. "I didn't know!" she cried. "He never told me! I knew he was saving, but I had no idea how much. Four hundred! I just can't believe it!"

"He was a secret man," Janet wound up her expressions of wonder. "You couldn't ever tell what he was thinking. Just fancy all that money and never a word about it!"

"Well, it looks as if it was Edith's now," Trimble declared. "I'll borrow this book. But you needn't be afraid, Edith, I'm not going to steal the money. Couldn't if I wanted to," he added regretfully. "Now that's all. I'll look into the thing and let you know further."

James Trimble was a rising man in his service. His superintendent had a high opinion of him, and though he had been pleased at his recent promotion, he did not intend to let him stop at sergeant. When therefore on the Wednesday morning Trimble asked for an interview the super received him without hesitation.

"What's it now, Jimmy?" he asked, pointing to a chair. It was only on formal occasions that the young man was Sergeant Trimble.

"I heard something last night, sir, and I think you should know about it. I was up at Dr Marsham's. I know the cook there and she sometimes asks me in. It's about the doctor's attendant, Joseph Rawlins," and he gave the superintendent an even clearer and more concise account of the affair than Edith's.

Superintendent Rider listened carefully. "The man has disappeared, the girl who is practically engaged to him throws doubt on the letter explaining the disappearance, and he has ostensibly gone to South America leaving £400 in the bank, which apparently neither of them can get."

"That's right, sir. I don't think he could get it without the book, or not from Brazil without a lot of trouble, and she would need a will and proof of his death."

"Exactly. Well, I admit it looks bad and you were quite right to tell me. Now here's what I'll do. I'll send the letter and the handwriting samples to the Yard. If the letter's okay I'll drop the thing: if it's a forgery I'll take it up." He paused and glanced at the obviously disappointed sergeant. "If I gave you today, do you think you could find out anything helpful?"

Trimble tried to hide his satisfaction. "I could try, sir," he answered modestly.

"Well, try. It would be useful if you could get an idea where Rawlins went to during his leave. How would he normally travel between the doctor's house and the town?"

"Bus, I should say, sir. Two services pass the end of the road."

"Likely enough. Then I suggest you try the conductors. You might find that he went to the railway or the coach

PART 2: THE BITERS BIT

station. The time he arrived might give you a likely train or coach."

Trimble was really grateful. This was a wonderful chance he was being given and the super was doing all he could to help him. Though he felt a day was too short to hope for much result, he thanked Rider sincerely. Perhaps if he showed results he would be given more time.

It occurred to him that he might get more from the conductors if he wore plain clothes, so he changed before going out. He began by calling on the bus manager, showing his credentials, explaining his commission, and asking for a list of conductors who worked on the routes in question. This he was presently handed.

Then began a long, tedious inquiry. First he had to find the men, no easy task. All the morning he worked without result. A quick lunch and he was at it again. By the evening he was sick and tired of the job. Then just as he was thinking he'd have to up and confess defeat, he struck oil.

A conductor came into the station to wait for his bus. Trimble introduced himself, and the man's name being on the list, began his questions. When he came to, "Do you happen to know a man named Rawlins? He's attendant to Dr Marsham up there at The Gables," his patience was rewarded.

"Yes, I know the chap," the conductor answered. "Dark gloomy sort of man without much to say. I live that way and I've met him in the local."

"I suppose he travels in and out by bus?"

"Well, he's been with me a few times, but of course I can't say he always goes that way."

"Has he travelled with you lately?"

Then came the wonderful words: "Strange you should ask me that, for he has. Last Saturday evening he was on the bus."

"Last Saturday? Saturday week, you mean?"

"Oh no, I don't. It was last Saturday on the eight-forty bus from the town. He got off at Dr Marsham's road just before nine."

Trimble's head whirled. "That's important to me, mate. I take it you're sure?"

"Of course I'm sure. I wouldn't say it if I wasn't."

"Where did he join you?"

"Ah, now you've got me." The man paused. "Let's see. I believe it was Central Station, though I couldn't say for certain. We pass Central Station on that run and I think it was there."

Trimble was so astonished by this information that he thought of going off then and there to report to Superintendent Rider. Then his training saved him.

"Anyone else on that bus who might have known Rawlins? If so, he might be sure about where he got on."

The conductor considered. "Yes, there was. Man called Truescott, a farmer. Goes to the local too. I remember now I saw him speak to Rawlins as he took his seat."

Half an hour later Trimble was knocking at Truescott's door. The conductor's recollection was correct. Rawlins had got in at the station on the previous Saturday evening. Truescott distinctly remembered seeing him.

It was with enthusiasm that Sergeant Trimble made his report next morning. Rider heard him in silence. "Not bad at all," he commented when the recital was ended. "Keep that sort of thing up and you'll do. Now this is growing interesting. Rawlins was going back at the time he was expected, but between the bus stop and Dr Marsham's house something happened to him. How far is that by the way?"

PART 2: THE BITERS BIT

"The stop's at the end of the road, sir. The house is about three hundred yards down it."

"He'd walk it in three or four minutes. Quite a problem. Did you ask if anyone else got out at the stop?"

Trimble felt his little bubble of complacency go flat. "Well no, sir, I'm afraid I didn't," he stammered.

"Never mind, you can't think of everything on the spur of the moment. Now you can have another whack at it tomorrow. Find that out if you can: if anyone else got out. If so, go and see them. Then try round for anyone in the neighbourhood who was out at the time. Call at the local houses. Someone may have seen Rawlins on the road. With luck you may get something."

Next morning Trimble went to work with a will, this time wearing his uniform. First he looked up his friends the bus conductor and Truescott. From them he learnt nothing more. Then ensued a longer and even more wearisome inquiry than that of the previous day. At each house at which he called – and he omitted none – he had to make elaborate explanations before he could even begin to ask his questions. Then when for the second time he was considering calling it a day, for the second time he struck oil.

Albert Giles, a boy of thirteen returning home from a visit to some friends, had passed along the road on the Saturday evening. After making a detailed timetable of his movements, Trimble was able to fix the time at about 8.55, five minutes before the Rawlins' bus was due. On the road was a car. It stood heading towards the main road near a path which led up to a well-known view point. Two men were in it. Giles had not seen their faces clearly as the nearest lamp was some distance away.

What make was the car? He couldn't tell. Nor had he noticed the number. All he could remember was that it was a post-war medium-sized saloon and that it wanted cleaning. When he had reached the end of the road he had looked back and it was still there.

"Come along, son, and show me just where it stood," Trimble invited.

The boy was thrilled. Trimble made a careful search for tyre marks, unfortunately without success.

This information opened up a new vista. Was the car connected with the affair? Could these men have been waiting for Rawlins and have driven him away? If so, did Rawlins go with them willingly or under compulsion? Trimble thought over it late into the night, but without reaching a conclusion.

Next morning he found that Superintendent Rider had developed a more lively interest in the case. A reply had come from Scotland Yard about the Brazilian letter. The experts unhesitatingly declared it a forgery. They had found on it, moreover, five different sets of fingerprints. These they had photographed, but they pointed out that none of them necessarily belonged to the writer.

"Yours among them?" asked the superintendent with a glint of humour in his eye.

Trimble, embarrassed, admitted regretfully that this indeed might be so. "I know, sir, that four people handled it after it was delivered. Dr Marsham opened it and threw it into the waste-paper basket. Edith Jones, the housemaid, got it out and handed it to the cook, Janet Proctor, and Janet handed it to me."

"Four people? Are you sure only four?"

Trimble hesitated. "I only know of three besides myself, sir, but of course I can't be certain that neither Miss Parratt nor Miss Kelso touched it."

PART 2: THE BITERS BIT

"The fifth might be one of those two, I suppose, or with luck it might be the writer. We'll have to check up on those prints. You may go again to The Gables and get samples from everyone."

"Yes, sir." Trimble again tried to hide his satisfaction.

"You'll have to be careful," went on Rider. "You can't demand prints and they can refuse to give them. But if you explain, politely why they're wanted, you'll probably have no trouble. In fact, you'd better tell the doctor in confidence what's in the wind. It shouldn't look as if we were acting behind his back."

"Yes, sir."

"It'll be enough to ask the ladies did they handle the paper. If they say not accept their word and don't bother them further."

"I understand, sir," said Trimble, who would have acted in this way in any case.

"Since the letter's a forgery I'm afraid we'll have to go all out on the case. How did you get on yesterday?"

Rider was more impressed by the news of the car than Trimble expected. "Hard to believe there's no connection," he commented. "Here you have a man mysteriously disappearing during a four-minute walk, and then you find that just before he arrived a car was waiting on that very stretch. My bet is he went in the car."

"Willingly or unwillingly, sir?"

"Ah, now you're talking. On the face of it I should say unwillingly. If it had been otherwise he'd surely have called and seen the girl Jones."

Trimble was emphatic. "Certainly, sir, he'd have seen Miss Jones."

"Then there's the letter. Since it was forged the story's presumably false, and if so, it had compulsion written all over it. That's not proved of course, but till we know more I'm assuming that Rawlins was murdered and by the men in the car."

"It certainly looks like it."

The super bent forward. "Now, Jimmy, I'm going to disappoint you, but when you think it over you'll see I can't do anything else. You've done good work these last two days, but I can't put you in charge. You're too young and you haven't got enough experience."

Trimble had realized this was too much to hope for. "I didn't expect it, sir," he answered quietly.

"That's right. Well, I may tell you between ourselves that none of us can handle the thing. With Inspector Ross ill and Inspector Christie busy with that Archer case we've no one to do it. I'm going to recommend calling in the Yard. The CC's fond of the Yard and he'll certainly agree."

This decision set in motion a well-established sequence of events. An application received at the Yard was passed to Chief Superintendent French. It happened that no chief inspector was available to take over the case and French decided to entrust it to Inspector Rollo, a young product of the Hendon College who had assisted him on previous occasions. With surprise and delight Rollo heard that he was immediately to accompany his chief to Folkestone, prepared to stay there several nights. Within the hour they had set off and in due course were seated with Rider in his office.

It was no longer French's habit to undertake outside inquiries like this one. But at the beginning of cases he frequently went to find out what they were about and to start a subordinate on the right road. Particularly was this the case when the subordinate was a junior. He was glad to give Rollo this chance. The young man had made good

PART 2: THE BITERS BIT

since his promotion, but he had not had a great deal of experience and it was clear that a little guidance would not come amiss. French explained the position to Rider.

"I'll stay myself for a day or two to start the inquiry," he went on, "and will come down frequently to keep track of things, but Inspector Rollo will be in charge under you. I'll send a sergeant to help him when I'm away."

"Very good, Mr French. That'll suit us and of course we'll give you all the help we can. We have a young sergeant here, Trimble, who had been working on the case. Indeed, it was he who first suspected something wrong. If he'd be any use to Inspector Rollo he's welcome to have him full time. I don't want to wish him on you, but he's a local and knows the place and the people, including the missing man."

"That might do very well, Mr Rider. I think if you don't mind we must leave it to Rollo."

"Of course: only reasonable. Now the case so far is this," and Rider gave the details of what had happened. Then he called in Trimble, who explained his part, ending up: "I got those prints, sir, Dr Marsham's, the housemaid's, the cook's and my own. Neither of the ladies had handled the letter."

"It sounds as if there'd be a bit of work in it," French commented. "If I may say so, Mr Rider, you people haven't lost much time. Now I'd like to fix up rooms for a night or two, and then if you can spare the sergeant I'd like to go out to The Gables and meet the people we've been hearing about."

– 10 –

THE RAMSGATE PASSENGER

French was pleased with his reception at Folkestone. This Rider seemed a good chap who would help without unduly interfering. And young Trimble promised well. It might indeed be wise for Rollo to choose him as his assistant. The man's local knowledge might prove useful, but on the other hand Rollo might want the superior technical help of a sergeant from the Yard. French would not coerce the young fellow, but he thought a gentle hint would not be out of place.

The three officers called at an hotel and then drove to The Gables. Marsham had been thinking over what Trimble had told him. He was obviously horrified at the suggestion of murder and ready to argue that the idea was absurd. "I agree that Superintendent Rider must think very seriously of the affair to have called in the Yard," he conceded, "but who could have wanted to kill a man like Rawlins? He was quiet and inoffensive and certainly not one to make enemies."

"Well, sir, you may be right. But where there's suspicion we have to look into it."

"Oh yes, I see that. And of course if any of us can help, we'll be glad to do so."

Marsham then told what he knew of Rawlins, including an account of the journey to Zürich and the man's request

PART 2: THE BITERS BIT

for leave. He was of a taciturn and somewhat gloomy disposition but he understood the doctor and was always careful and efficient. The doctor was sorry to lose him and hoped he had come to no harm.

Julia Parratt was also anxious to help, but she was unable to supply further details. French therefore turned to Nancy. He was impressed by her good will and felt that she was anything but a fool, but there was a hesitation in her manner that puzzled him. He could see that the Swiss trip had made a deep impression on her, and she told in more detail of its origin, of the visit to the Stour to inspect Dolbey's tidal turbine, of seeing and going over the launch and of the runs to and from Basle. "See," she went on, handing him a folder, "here's the cruise itinerary. Of course we didn't take all those excursions, but it'll give you an idea what the thing was like."

French took it with thanks. None of this particularly interested him, but when he asked his next routine question he began to wonder if he had got something.

"Now, you've been with Dr Marsham for a considerable time and you've seen Rawlins during all of it. Tell me, was there any occasion on which he seemed surprised or excited or pleased or upset without apparent reason?"

At this Nancy hesitated. "Well," she said at last, "there was such an occasion, but I don't like to speak of it because I may so easily have been mistaken. The signs he showed were very slight."

"Tell me all the same."

"It was just after we reached Zürich. Dr Marsham had left some papers on the launch and he sent Rawlins back to Kaiseraugst to get them. He left about eleven in the evening and should have been back not later than about three in the morning. But he didn't turn up until ten. He said he had lost his way in the dark and had slept in the car."

"Yes, Dr Marsham mentioned that. What was the special point which struck you?"

"Merely Rawlins' manner. I thought he seemed excited when he returned and rather pleased with himself. And different times at Zurich and on the way home, and indeed since we reached home, I've seen him when he thought he wasn't observed, smiling and looking, as it were, triumphant. I don't express it very well."

"On the contrary, Miss Kelso, you express it admirably. He said nothing to indicate what had pleased him?"

"Nothing."

Though French admired what he saw of Nancy, he was not altogether satisfied with her evidence. She seemed uneasy, indeed frightened. Some timid people did show alarm when being questioned by the police, but she did not strike him as of this type. Rather she gave him the impression that she was keeping something back, or more likely, that she could not make up her mind whether she should or should not mention it. He suggested this to her, but she strenuously denied any such misgivings. On the whole he felt he might be mistaken as he could find no fault with the way she answered his questions.

Edith Jones, whom he took next, had seen the change in Rawlins, but she was sure he had also been perplexed and anxious. She had ragged him, saying he had clearly fallen for some Swiss skirt, but he only grew sulky and told her not to be silly. She explained that they would probably have shortly become engaged and repeated his remark about coming into money.

Janet Proctor being unable to add to his information, French went on to examine Rawlins' room. In view of

PART 2: THE BITERS BIT

Nancy's statement he was interested to find a copy of Loxton's folder of the Rhine trips. He turned to Trimble.

"You didn't mention this in your report?"

"Well no, sir. I didn't think it was important. It seemed to me reasonable that he'd want to keep a memento of the trip."

French had been turning over the leaves. "I dare say you're right," he returned. "All the same I'll slip it into my case. I notice that certain items are marked."

He had taken a mental note to search for fingerprints in Rawlins' room in the hope of identifying the fifth print on the letter. While he went through the papers, he set Rollo and Trimble to work on this, at the same time phoning Rider for a photographer. The job took a considerable time, but at the end a large number of prints had been brought up. They found also spaces where prints had been wiped out. These spaces were themselves print shaped and they showed that someone in gloves had been over the room. The photographer remained behind to make the necessary records.

Before leaving, French glanced again at Loxton's folder. The prices charged staggered him. £30 a week for four weeks meant for the doctor's party £480: quite a sum for ten days in Zürich. When seeing the doctor on the way out he happened to mention that Loxton knew how to charge.

"Oh well," said Marsham, "I didn't pay that. He took us for £300. It was because we went straight through and didn't take day excursions. Also the launch lay up for an extra week in Switzerland."

As he spoke he was fumbling in one of the drawers of his desk. "I have the folder here," he went on, "and you can see what the individual day trips cost." He continued to search.

"Funny thing, I could have sworn it was in this drawer, but it's not there now. One of the girls must have taken it."

French was suddenly interested. "Tell me, sir, was your copy marked in any way?"

"Yes, I put a note to certain excursions which I thought we might take in spite of our hurry."

"That it, sir?"

Dr Marsham stared at him. "Why yes," he exclaimed. "Those are my marks. Where did you get it?"

"In Rawlins' desk."

"Rawlins! What could he have wanted with it? I certainly shouldn't have suspected him of searching my desk."

"Probably only a memento," French said smoothly. "It wouldn't be altogether unreasonable."

French now thought they had obtained all the information required at the moment. Having thanked the doctor, he and his companions took their leave.

"Now let's see," he remarked, "it's getting late. I expect if we want any dinner we'd better go and have it. What about you, Sergeant? We'd be pleased if you'd join us for tonight."

Trimble flushed with pleasure. "That's extremely good of you, sir," he declared. "I'd greatly like to."

During the meal French chatted pleasantly on various subjects, but as they sat over coffee he returned to the business in hand. "Now, Rollo," he demanded, "you're running this show. What do you make of all we've learnt?"

Rollo seemed slightly embarrassed. Then he made a quick movement as if to shake off what might be a handicap. When he spoke it was clearly and with some decision.

"It seems to me, sir, that Rawlins had intended returning to the doctor's until he left the bus, but at the last moment he changed his mind or was prevented. It looks as if the men in the car were waiting for him and that he went away with them. I should say that he was probably forced to do so, but I don't think that is actually proved."

"The forged letter?" put in French.

"If he had wished to disappear, owing perhaps to something the men told him, the forged letter might have been part of the trick, but I admit that in this case I should have expected him to write it himself."

"Very well. Go on."

"From his remark to Edith Jones it looks as if he expected to come in for some money during his leave. He had been excited, anxious and nervous which suggests that everything might not have been plain sailing. Possibly he was contemplating a crime, a burglary or some form of swindling. At a guess, sir, the men might have been accomplices and they might have learnt something which made the flight of all three necessary. Or the crime might have injured them only and they might have got him in revenge." Rollo suddenly smiled. "I expect, sir, I'm talking through my hat."

"I expect so," French agreed pleasantly. "All the same carry on. Anything else?"

"Yes, there's another point. Rawlins' change of manner at Zürich and his getting hold of the folder suggests a connection with the Swiss trip, but I can't think what it might have been."

"Yes, I agree with you there. Not too bad, Rollo. Anything to add to that, Sergeant?"

Trimble seemed surprised to be included in the discussion. "No, sir," he answered tactfully, "I think what the Inspector said covers everything. There's perhaps one point. Owing to my knowing Rawlins and Edith Jones, I should think it unlikely that he went off voluntarily with the men. I feel sure that if he could he would have gone in first to see Edith."

"Even if the men had told him he was in danger of arrest?"

"I think so, sir. He needn't have stayed."

"It's a point, Sergeant, and we'll keep it in view. Now, Rollo, what would you do next?"

"Rawlins got into the bus at the Central Station. I think I'd go there and see what trains arrived about that time."

French nodded his approval. "Good. That's what I hoped you'd say. Job for tomorrow."

Presently they had final drinks in the bar. When a little later Trimble went home Rollo had reached a decision on at least one problem.

"If you agree, sir, I'd like to work with that chap. He seems easy to get on with and no fool."

"That's principally what I asked him to dinner for," French returned: "to give you a chance to make up your mind. I think you're probably right. He's not Police College, is he?"

"No, sir, but he's all right."

"I like your 'but'."

Rollo grinned. "Well, sir, he knows this place and the doctor's household and the missing man. I think that might be useful."

Next morning, French and Rollo had a formal meeting with the Chief Constable, who seemed pleased that Trimble had been chosen as Rollo's helper. "He's not a bad young fellow," he considered, "and of course he's got Superintendent Rider behind him. Between them you'll get all the help that we can give." French thanked him and after good wishes from the CC the brief interview ended.

PART 2: THE BITERS BIT

As they left the room the photographer appeared. "I've got the records of those fingerprints, sir," he said, handing over three lots of cards. "These were taken yesterday in Rawlins' room at The Gables, these others are the prints of those living in the house, and this third lot are what the Yard found on the Brazil letter."

"Right, Constable. You've come at a good time," French told him. "I'm just ready for them."

French laid the photographs out on a table in the room which had been put at their disposal. First he took those of the prints found in Rawlins' room. These he numbered, and selecting the first, began searching for it among those from the occupants of The Gables. He presently found it. Having made sure of the identification with his lens, he was able to say that it had been made by Edith Jones' right forefinger.

The next he could not trace, nor the next, but the fourth was Trimble's. So he went on, working through them in his slow painstaking way. The process was tedious, but he kept at it till at last all those found in the room, had been gone over.

The result he considered eminently satisfactory. The large number of unidentified prints, some of them duplicated several times, could, he was satisfied, belong only to Rawlins. This conclusion was confirmed by the fact that the prints were found on articles which only Rawlins was likely to have handled, such as the interior pages of his bank book. French called it a morning and with the others went out to lunch.

On resuming work he took the letter. The different prints found on it had been numbered by the Yard, and these numbers had been marked on two sheets of tracing paper, for the front and back respectively. When the sheets were placed over the letter the numbers fell on the corresponding prints.

ANYTHING TO DECLARE?

French now repeated his work of the morning. Taking No. 1 print on the letter, he began searching for it among those from The Gables. Soon he found it was Dr Marsham's. Once again progress was painfully slow, but he worked doggedly on till at last the job was finished.

He found himself well repaid for his trouble. The letter had been handled by Marsham, Edith, Janet, Trimble – and Rawlins!

The discovery shook French. He found himself plunged once more into doubt. If Rawlins' prints were on the letter, had the man not written it? And if so, had he not gone on the Continent with his Brazilian employer?

Only for a moment did French consider this. Quite apart from the Yard testimony about forgery, he saw that he had, if not proof, at least strong evidence that the story was false. The £400! Was it conceivable that if Rawlins had intended to go to Brazil, and had been practically at the house on that Saturday night, that he would not have gone in to get the bank book which would have enabled him to withdraw it? French did not know whether without the book he could have got the money, but he was sure it could not be done quickly or easily. He took a note to find out. In the meantime he felt they might definitely assume that Rawlins was dead.

Therefore his work with the fingerprints must be completed. Slipping two other pieces of tracing paper over those sent from the Yard, he marked on them all the prints known to be Rawlins'. These he began to study. If Rawlins had handled the letter, would the prints fall in just those places and directions?

One point struck him immediately. In no single case did a print on the front of the letter register with one on the back. Rawlins therefore had not once picked the sheet up

PART 2: THE BITERS BIT

or handled it. All the prints must have been made by touching it as it lay on a flat surface.

This was significant and his second discovery was not less so. All the prints were of isolated fingers, pressed down without relation to any other. Rawlins' hand had not rested on the paper.

French sat back, deeply interested. It looked as if the prints had not been made naturally. If so, it surely followed that Rawlins had not himself made them: someone else had pressed his fingers on to the paper. The operator had not known enough to make a convincing job.

Here, French felt, was further confirmation, if further confirmation was needed, of murder. With a mind at last free from doubt on this essential issue, he felt he could carry on with more confidence. Rollo and Trimble, who had watched the demonstration with feelings approaching awe, were enthusiastic. They didn't presume to congratulate him, but he saw that the wish to do so was in their minds.

He would have liked a breathing space after his work, but there was another job which he felt must be tackled without delay: Rawlins' movements. "We'll have a word with that stationmaster," he decided. "Just ring him up that we're coming."

Ten minutes later they were in the man's office. Rollo, who had been told to conduct the interview, began by confidentially explaining their business and asking for his help. The stationmaster, pleased by this approach, promised to do his best. Rollo then put his question.

"What trains arrived on Saturday just before the 8.50 bus left?" repeated the stationmaster. "That's an easy one. The express from London: leaves Charing Cross 7.15, arrives here 8.40. Ten minutes would give more than enough time to catch the bus."

"That would seem to suit. It is the only train about that time?"

"No, there's an up train also. Leaves Ramsgate at 7.25 and gets here at 8.43. Seven minutes would still be plenty of time for the bus."

"Then our man might be coming from almost anywhere," Rollo smiled. "Could you tell us if those trains were on time last Saturday evening?"

"The signalman will know." The stationmaster picked up his telephone. There were questions and murmured replies. "Both exactly on time that night," he declared, adding with a smile, "I'm afraid we're not always able to give so satisfactory a reply."

Rollo smiled in his turn and said that from the police point of view it would have been better if one of them had arrived after the bus had left. Then he thanked the stationmaster and made as to withdraw. But with a twinkle in his eye French shook his head. He turned to the stationmaster.

"There's just one other question we'd like to ask if you'd be so kind. The man we're trying to trace left Folkestone on the previous Saturday, the 17th. Presumably on that day he took a monthly return ticket. Can you tell us whether the return half of a ticket – it will certainly be a third – issued on the 17th, was collected off either of those trains on last Saturday?"

"Ah," said the stationmaster, "you have me there. I can't tell you that. But they could at headquarters. I'll ring them up now if you like, but this being Saturday it's not likely that there'll be a reply till Monday. That do?"

PART 2: THE BITERS BIT

"We're exceedingly obliged," French returned. "The sooner we hear the better of course, but Monday will do."

When they reached the car Rollo was apologetic. "I'm sorry, sir, I missed that point about the ticket. I should have thought of it."

"You should have," French agreed, "and no doubt you would have later. But to ask it then saved worrying the stationmaster a second time, which was better avoided."

It was now evening. French considered returning to London and leaving Rollo to carry on. Then he thought that the case had not yet been sufficiently developed. He stayed the night therefore at Folkestone. Next morning he was glad he had done so, for the stationmaster rang up.

"It just happens that some late work was being done last night," he explained, "and though it's Sunday I've got the reply to your question. Shall I tell you over the phone or will you call round?"

"Call round if it's the same to you." French was not keen on discussing his cases over the public wire.

The stationmaster greeted them as brothers when a little later they reached his office. "There were five return halves collected off those trains," he told them, "all issued the previous Saturday. Four of them were from London and one from Ramsgate. That what you wanted?"

"Yes, indeed," French agreed. "Most helpful. I suppose you could not tell us what trains they were issued for? We know the time our man left for the station."

The stationmaster shook his head. "I'm afraid not. There are no records that would give that now."

"From the time our man left his house and the length of the bus journey we think he reached the station about 2.55. That any help?"

"Why, yes," answered the stationmaster. "A train leaves for Ramsgate at 3.3 and for Victoria at 3.22. It looks like Ramsgate."

"Yes, because a later bus would have caught the other," French agreed and expressed his thanks. Privately he thought they had been exceptionally lucky.

"Well, Rollo," he went on when they had regained the car, "any more ideas?"

"One point, sir." Rollo spoke eagerly as if he thought his contribution valuable. "We suspected that Rawlins might have been interested in the launch trip. Well, according to the folder the launch sails from Ramsgate. And here we find someone travelled to and from Ramsgate on the days and at the hours Rawlins left and returned. Cumulative evidence, isn't it, sir?"

"You're right as far as you go. But you're hardly doing yourself justice, Rollo. Think again. Have we no further evidence on the point?"

Rollo suddenly became deflated. "I – I," he stammered. "I'm afraid I don't see what you mean."

"Look up the folder."

When they reached headquarters they got out the advertisement. As Rollo was poring over it French added: "See the running of the ship."

For some moments longer Rollo stared, then he slapped his thigh, "I've got it, sir! I don't know how I came to miss it. During that week the launch was there! It arrived at Ramsgate on the Saturday Rawlins began his leave and left on the day he returned. Between those days it was lying in the Stour."

French nodded. "That's it. The evidence still accumulates."

"I'll say it does! We might surely take that as a working basis?"

"As one of them at least. Then what do you suggest?"

"A visit to Ramsgate. Try and pick up something there."

"Very well, it's up to you. But you'll have to fix up first with the Super."

"Of course. And you, sir? You wouldn't think of coming to Ramsgate?"

"No, I've spoon-fed you enough. You're on your own now. In any case I must go back to town."

An hour later French was in the train.

– 11 –

THE CIVILIAN COLLEAGUE

As he leant back in his corner seat French's thoughts remained with Rollo and the case with which he had been entrusted. French was not altogether happy about his choice. Nothing against Rollo: he had done well in lesser jobs, he was young and he had to learn. But would the choice be considered favouritism? Rollo had been French's protégé, and though no one was likely to say anything, the belief that French had been swayed by his own preference might give rise to undesirable feelings.

But right or wrong, the thing was done. What French had now to see was that his choice was justified: that Rollo got his man. A little unobtrusive help seemed indicated.

He went on to reconsider the case. Though, as Rollo himself had pointed out, there was no absolute proof of foul play, French felt but little doubt that Rawlins had indeed been murdered. If so, the work done at Folkestone was satisfactory in that they had learnt a reasonable amount for the time expended. But it was not satisfactory in that it contained no pointer to the murderer. Moreover it was quite on the cards that Rollo's inquiries in Ramsgate would achieve nothing. For these reasons French felt that he must look on the affair as his own. It would be well to be in a position to give a hint to Rollo should the need arise.

PART 2: THE BITERS BIT

After a general review which produced no fresh ideas his thoughts turned to a point which had slightly puzzled him when it had been mentioned: the figure Dr Marsham had paid for his trip. The normal charge for four was £480, but Marsham had been taken for £300. The reason given was the saving on excursions and the launch's lying up in Switzerland for an extra week. He took out the folder lent by Nancy Kelso, which he had put in his case, and looked up the excursions. A little mathematics might clear up the matter.

First he totted up the cost of the excursions the Marsham party had taken. This amounted to £30. Then he found the total costs of all the excursions: it was £90. £30 from £90 left £60, which was the amount Loxton had saved on the excursions.

Next, to find the saving on the launch for the extra week lying up in Switzerland. This was more difficult, but a careful estimate indicated about £40. £40 on the launch and £60 on the excursions made a total saving of £100. But Loxton had taken them for £300, a reduction of £180!

Here was more than justification for French's doubts. Loxton must have had some very strong reason for wanting to get the doctor's party, if he let them off £80. It had seemed possible that Rawlins' disappearance was connected with the cruise, now French began to wonder if there could be something phoney about the cruise itself.

Scotland Yard has consultant experts on practically every subject, and next morning when he had gone through his letters French rang up one of these to arrange an interview. Mr Holden was the retired manager of a tourist agency and there was little about the business he did not know. French suggested calling at his house at Highgate.

"I'm just going down town," Holden answered. "If it suits I can be with you about ten."

It suited French admirably. He greeted Holden warmly and for some minutes they chatted with enthusiasm about their respective gardens. Then with a sigh French turned to business.

"Launch trips on the Rhine," he began, handing over Loxton's folder. "Know anything about that?"

"I've heard of it," Holden replied, "but I've never gone into it."

"Well, I want you to go into it now, from the financial side. I can tell you the point in a word. Is £480 for four people a fair figure for the trip?"

"I couldn't possibly answer that straight off, I'd have to work the thing out. But at a first glance it seems reasonable enough."

"Can you work it out here or shall you have to take it away?"

"Here. We've done these Rhine excursions times without number and I've a pretty fair idea what they cost. Also running launches."

"Good. Then there's a table and there's a chair and if you want anything else the whole of the Yard's behind you."

"Whisky and soda?"

"That afterwards."

"Right. I'll hold you to it."

For some time there was silence, then Holden threw down his pen. "I was right," he declared. "£480's a fair figure for what they undertake to do. That all you want?"

"Well, not exactly. One other point. A special trip was run for a party," and French described the Marsham itinerary. "That would come a bit cheaper to Loxton, wouldn't it?"

PART 2: THE BITERS BIT

"Oh yes, he'd save on the excursions and also a bit on the launch lying up longer."

"That's what I thought. Well look here, Holden, what reduction should he have made because of it?"

Holden picked up the folder. "According to the terms of this he wasn't bound to have made any. £30 per person per week is the cost of the standard trip. This may be modified to suit individual requirements, but there's nothing about an allowance for doing so."

"I follow. But supposing Loxton wished to give Marsham what benefits he could, perhaps to get them to book?"

"If he did that or if his conscience was working at high pressure he could have cut quite a bit and still made his profit."

"That's it. By how much could he have reduced his charge?"

Again there was silence as Holden figured. "Can't be absolutely accurate," he said presently, "but I should say from £90 to £100."

"It couldn't be as much, say, as £180?"

"Heavens, no! That would be paying the party to go."

So he had been right and there was something exceptional in the reduction. French puzzled over it, then he rang up an inspector.

"I want you, Deacon, to go to Butler's; you know, the tourist people in Piccadilly. Get yourself up as a prosperous manufacturer or anyone you can think of who has money. Show them this," and he handed over the Loxton folder, "and say you might be interested in a trip in the spring. When you've asked enough questions say that before you decide you'd like to talk to someone who's been. If they give you the name of Marsham say you heard of him, but that you understand he didn't take several of the excursions and you'd rather meet someone who had the standard itinerary. Got all that?"

In an hour Deacon was back. There had been some unwillingness to give the information, but the manager, appealed to, had said: "Give him Sir Harvey Arbuthnot's name. He was very pleased with the trip and he won't mind saying so."

Sir Harvey Arbuthnot was a well-known barrister whom French had met more than once in court. This was satisfactory in a way, as French would be sure of a ready hearing and accurate information. But with Sir Harvey he could not work the prospective traveller dodge. He would get what he wanted only if he put all his cards on the table.

He rang him up and made an appointment for that evening. When he arrived at the house in Hampstead Sir Harvey had just finished dinner and was having coffee in his study.

"Just in time for a cup, Mr French," he said pleasantly.

While they were drinking it he chatted of a forgery case in which both had been engaged, then when the cups had been removed he went on: "Well, you haven't come to talk of ancient history. What can I do for you this evening?"

"It's a very small thing, sir, and I hardly like to apply to you, for I'm working on the merest suspicion."

"In other words it's a confidential matter. Right, I understand."

French smiled. "Thank you. I believe you were on one of these Rhine cruises?" and he produced the folder.

"Yes, that's right. What of it?"

"A rather impertinent question, I'm afraid. It's about the cost. The folder says £30 per week per person. The question is, were you charged that amount?"

PART 2: THE BITERS BIT

Sir Harvey looked interested. "That tells me you've got something up your sleeve. As a matter of fact we were not charged the full figure. Butler's people said that Captain Loxton would be glad to take us at a reduction, as the venture was just starting and our names would make a useful advertisement."

"Would it be indiscreet to ask the amount of the reduction?"

"Not at all. He reduced his £30 a week to £20."

"That's quite a bit. Was it suggested, sir, that your party would not go unless it was made?"

"No, it was Loxton's suggestion. But admittedly I was hesitating when it was made."

French was impressed. Here was conclusive evidence that there was something phoney about the trips. From what Holden had said, Loxton could not accept two-thirds of his advertised figure without suffering a heavy loss. He decided to take the barrister into his full confidence.

"I'll tell you the point, Sir Harvey. One of the members of the last party, the attendant of an invalid doctor, has disappeared under circumstances pointing to foul play. In trying to find a motive we naturally considered the trip. Incidentally we found that the doctor was taken at a rate which must have meant a heavy loss to Loxton. This suggested there was more about the trip than met the eye. Now you have practically confirmed that."

Sir Harvey was watching him keenly.

"So now," French went on, "I'd like to ask you the further question, did you notice anything suspicious or out of the way while you were on board?"

"That's all very interesting, Mr French. I have to admit that I did not. Everything seemed normal and above-board."

They had some further conversation and after drinks French took his leave.

From what he had heard two things seemed clear: one, that Loxton was extremely anxious to fill his launch on these trips, two, that this was not for the money he made out of the passengers. If then the trips weren't paying, why was he running them? Could they be profitable in some other way? If so, how? Could they be – ? Ah, could that be it? Could these people be smuggling?

The idea was supported by the fact that the launch lay empty of passengers for some nights at each end of the journey, perfect opportunities for loading and unloading contraband. The more French thought over it, the more likely it seemed.

Then it occurred to him that he was on the wrong track. What if these people were smuggling? Very reprehensible no doubt, but no business of his. What he wanted was to help Rollo in the Rawlins case. The cruise was nothing to him.

And yet was it not? He remembered Rawlins' activities after reaching Switzerland: a visit to the launch, unexpected and at night, absence for the whole night instead of a few hours, a subsequent air of excitement and jubilation. Certainly suggestive. What if during that night Rawlins saw more than was good for him? And following that, what if he had been murdered for it?

Next morning French took out once again the cruise folder. The launch was due to leave Ramsgate Pier at 6.00 p.m. on Saturday, the Saturday of Rawlins' disappearance. Loxton and Edgley were presumably on board. If so, they were innocent of the murder. Who then could be guilty?

It was obvious that if smuggling were in progress, others beside those two must be involved. It was unlikely that Loxton or Edgley could obtain in Switzerland contraband

PART 2: THE BITERS BIT

articles. There must surely be a local agent for this. Equally a distributing centre in this country would be called for. Almost certainly there must be two other partners and perhaps more.

If so, his next step must be to trace them. It would then be worth finding out where they were at nine on that Saturday evening.

But first as to Loxton and Edgley. He put through a call to police headquarters in Ramsgate. Would Rollo find out at what hour the *Komforta* sailed on the Saturday evening, and whether captain and crew were on board.

A couple of hours later there was a reply. The *Komforta* had left the wharf at six-fifteen and had anchored in the harbour. She had lain there all night and put to sea about eight on Sunday morning. Loxton and Edgley had left with her, but whether they had remained on board all the evening Rollo had not been able so far to find out.

So those two were in England at the fateful hour. Did that mean that they might be guilty after all? It seemed to French unlikely. The passengers would never stand for being left alone on the ship, particularly on their first night. Besides they had to be given dinner. Edgley alone might perhaps have managed everything, but there were two in the car on the doctor's road, so even if Loxton had been there he had an unknown companion. On the whole French thought it likely that Loxton and Edgley were innocent of the murder, but that they had associates who were guilty.

For a time he felt up against it. There did not seem to be any way in which to learn about the associates, if indeed they existed. In his mind he turned over one line of investigation after another without clearly seeing his way. At last he decided that the most promising – or more accurately the least unpromising – inquiry might be into the cruises. Were they indeed for smuggling? If so, what was being brought in and how could it be proved?

He rang up the investigation department of the Customs and asked for Mr Trent. "Hullo, Bob," he greeted a familiar voice. "Haven't seen you for ages. How goes it?"

Apparently it went well and French continued. "Look, Bob, I've a spot of trouble and I'd like to unload it on you. Can I see you if I go round now?"

Trent agreed with apparent alacrity. He greeted French warmly on his arrival and they talked for a few moments of past cases on which both had been engaged. Then French went on to put his problem.

"You interest me enormously," Trent answered. "As a matter of fact we've just become suspicious that Swiss watches are coming into the country more freely than is wholesome. But we've no idea how. Now you think you're on to smuggling from Switzerland. No wonder I'm interested."

"I'm not interested in smuggling," French returned, "except in the hope of it throwing light on my murder case. All the same I was wondering if we could join forces? Unofficially, of course."

Trent was enthusiastic. There was nothing he would like better. The matter was quickly settled.

"From what you say it's obvious that if there's smuggling the loading is done during those three days in Switzerland when those men have the launch to themselves," Trent began, "and similarly the unloading while lying up in the Stour."

"We've got more than that," French returned. "If our theory about Rawlins is correct the loading was done on the

PART 2: THE BITERS BIT

night of arrival at Kaiseraugst, and it's more than likely to be the same in the Stour."

"Then what about keeping a watch on those nights?"

"I'm for it," said French, "but I thought it would be more a job for you than for me."

"Where is the launch now?"

"Let's see – today's Tuesday. She left Ramsgate last Saturday week or rather early Sunday morning. She's due in Basle about six next Saturday evening, the 7th. When she discharges her passengers she goes on up to Kaiseraugst, where she lies Sunday, Monday and Tuesday. We don't know exactly where, but she must be easy to find since Rawlins did it."

"Do we know he did or is it only an assumption?"

"We know because he got the doctor's papers from on board."

"True. I'd forgotten that."

"Then the launch should reach Ramsgate on Friday night, the 20th. She lies all night in the harbour and sets down the passengers early Saturday morning. Presumably she then goes to the Stour. The unloading should be done that night."

"We'll get them in Switzerland," Trent declared decisively. "As you can imagine, we're well in with the Swiss Customs people. They'll put their men on to it. I expect they'd do the whole thing for us if we asked them."

French shook his head. "No, Bob, that won't do. I thought of it first thing, but it's no good."

"Why not?"

"Well, see what would happen. You'd get Loxton and Edgley and stop the smuggling – always assuming there is smuggling. If you do, you can't keep it secret: even if you tried, the returning passengers would blow the gaff. So the people over here at the distributing end get to know and they vanish."

"That's so, I suppose."

"Now you want those distributors to complete your case. But you don't want them as much as I want them. I believe that Loxton and Edgley are innocent of Rawlins' murder and I believe the distributors are guilty."

"That certainly makes a difference."

"So you see I must get those people and I can only do it through the cruise. I told you, Bob, that's why I've come to you."

Trent nodded. "I see your point. But look, Joe, I do think we should have them watched at Kaiseraugst. The Swiss people would arrange it if we asked them and they're very efficient. I assure you the launch people would know nothing about it."

"I don't like it."

"You needn't have the slightest fear. I'll tell you, I'll slip over to Switzerland myself and join in the operation. I'll guarantee no suspicion is aroused."

French was still not too happy about it, but he wanted Trent's help and he feared that if he made difficulties he might lose it. So he agreed. Trent was to get in touch with the Swiss authorities and to undertake with them the entire affair.

When French returned to the Yard a further idea struck him. He had been insistent that the fact that they were under suspicion must be kept from Loxton and Edgley. But what if Rollo's activities would give this vital fact away to the distributors?

It would be better, he thought, to incur a charge of inefficiency than to risk losing the quarry. He picked up his telephone and made two calls. The first was to Ramsgate:

PART 2: THE BITERS BIT

would they please instruct Rollo to drop everything and return forthwith to Folkestone. The second was to Folkestone: could Superintendent Rider see him if he went down by the next train? Both replies were satisfactory.

Later in the day French was once again seated with his two assistants in Rider's room. First he heard of Rollo's activities. The young man had been exceptionally discreet. The only person he had applied to was the Ramsgate harbour-master, and him he had asked to treat his questions confidentially. French decided that no harm to his plan had resulted.

He then reported what he himself had done and the conclusion he had reached. Rider did not seem pleased.

"You want to postpone work on the case for three or four weeks?" he said doubtfully. "Surely if we do that any clues there may be will be gone."

"I want more," said French. "I want you to drop the case completely. I want someone in your service to be guilty of an indiscretion to the newspapers: that the police are satisfied that Rawlins has gone to Brazil and that no crime has been committed."

"You're not asking much."

"Nothing less will prevent the distributors taking cover."

"The distributors?"

"I mean the shore members of the smuggling scheme, the persons who I believe committed the murder."

"I see your point, Mr French, and I admit it's sound. But it won't do us much good here."

"Why so?"

"Well, what do you think? We go into the thing and then we drop it and say no murder was committed. A little later you arrest the murderers. We'll look nice fools then, won't we?"

French considered this. "Your indiscreet representative can say it's what the officer from Scotland Yard has concluded. You think he's talking through his hat, but he's in charge and it's his pigeon. Then you can take credit for sending Sergeant Trimble to be in at the death – of course assuming I'm right and we find the murderers."

Rider laughed. "After that I don't see that I can say any more. But before taking steps we must consult the CC. It'll only be a matter of form, he'll agree to whatever you recommend."

Over this part of the programme at least there was no delay. It happened that a few minutes later Major Hope called at headquarters. Rider at once brought French and Rollo to his room and French stated his case. The CC appeared impressed and agreed without demur. Satisfied with the success of his diplomacy, French returned with Rollo to London.

– 12 –

THE MULTIPLE ARRESTS

The meetings with Superintendent Rider and Major Hope were on the Tuesday. On the Thursday there was a brief note from Trent that he was leaving that evening for Switzerland. As the launch was not to be interfered with while abroad, it seemed unlikely that there would be any further move in the case till her return on the Friday fortnight. French therefore sent Rollo to another job and settled down to grapple with his own somewhat neglected correspondence.

It soon became apparent that he had misjudged the situation. On the Monday a telegram arrived. It had been handed in at Zürich early that morning and read:

MEET ME WITHOUT FAIL THIS MONDAY EVENING AT PRIMROSE HOTEL CANTERBURY STOP SUGGEST BRING ROLLO AND TRIMBLE STOP URGENT TRENT.

French read the message with mixed feelings. This was an unexpected request. It could surely only mean that Trent had located the other members of the conspiracy. If so, it was of course all to the good. But how could he have obtained such information unknown to Loxton and Edgley? French also could not help deploring in any such discovery his own undistinguished part.

But if there was doubt about Trent's proceedings, there was none about his own. He would have to go. Moreover he would have to take Rollo and Trimble. No doubt it was a matter on which the AC should be consulted, though he felt that this was merely a matter of form. He rang up and asked for an interview.

Sir Mortimer Ellison was interested. Of course French must go, and if the Customs Department had solved one of their own problems, there was no reason why the CID should not benefit from it. "We've helped them often enough in the past," he went on. "It's about time they paid back some of their debt."

French was pleased with this view of the affair and more confidently made his arrangements with Rollo and Superintendent Rider. Thinking that a car might be useful, he drove to Canterbury. By seven he and his two juniors sat down to dinner at the Primrose Hotel. Trent had not arrived, but about nine he walked in. He took no notice of French at first and did his business at the reception desk. Then glancing round he seemingly caught sight of him, stopped and enacted the unexpected meeting of an old friend. They chatted for a couple of minutes during which Trent contrived to whisper, "Room 32 in fifteen minutes". Then with a breezy "I'll be seeing you" he disappeared upstairs.

French then gave an exhibition of the bored visitor in a strange town and discoursed with the hall porter on the local theatres and cinemas. One by one the three men drifted upstairs, meeting at the appointed time and place.

It was a private sitting-room and Trent explained that he had reserved it because they wanted some place to talk. "And, Joe, old man," he went on, "we've got something to talk about. Yes, things have been happening since we met."

"You're on to the receivers?"

PART 2: THE BITERS BIT

"I'm on to the receivers and now it's time you put in your oar. But I'd better tell you the whole thing as it happened."

French wanted to ask some leading questions, but he controlled his curiosity. Trent had brought in whisky and cigarettes and not till his guests were well provided did he begin his story.

"As you know, I fixed up a meeting with the Swiss authorities and when I got to Basle I found a Herr Schneider waiting for me. He was a good fellow, pleasant and easy to work with and anything but a fool. He listened to my story – that is, to your story – and then began telephoning. First he rang up the river authorities at Kaiseraugst and found out where the *Komforta* usually lay. It was off the small boat-slip of a private house, rented by a Mr Furnell, an Englishman. Captain Loxton paid the river people for mooring and they presumed he also paid Furnell for the use of the slip."

"A suggestive beginning," French observed. "Lying off an Englishman's ground."

"There's more to follow. Schneider then rang up the Kaiseraugst police. It seems in Switzerland the police know all about everyone." There was the suspicion of a wink in Trent's eye as he looked at French.

"So do we," French declared.

"Is that so? I'll take your word for it. Well, this Furnell was a newcomer. He'd rented the house and garden some six months earlier. That suggestive too?"

"I'll say so," French agreed. "The first trip of the launch was in April this year and they must have got ready for it some time before. Yes, it's working in all right."

"Furnell is unmarried and has a daily woman to do the house and cook his supper. He gets his own breakfast and is from home during the day."

"Did you find out where he went to?"

"That naturally was what I asked. Schneider said they couldn't tell me offhand, but they'd make inquiries and let me know."

"By the way, when did all this take place?"

"Last Friday. I travelled overland on Thursday night."

"And the launch was due in Basle on the Saturday evening?"

"That's right. Well, I need hardly say Schneider and I were there to see it arrive. It drew in to a little wharf and two men and two women came ashore with some luggage. A car was waiting and they drove off. The launch then went on upstream."

"Just what the other passengers described."

"Yes. Well, Schneider had a car and we ran out to Kaiseraugst. There we watched the launch come in sight and drop anchor before a small cottage. Schneider left me on guard and disappeared. Presently he came back with another man whom he introduced as Herr Lehner of the River Police.

" 'Our friends have taken this matter very seriously,' said Schneider, and he pointed to a launch moored about a hundred yards upstream. 'That's one of their boats. They'll watch what goes on during the day and they suggest that we clear out till dark. Tonight we'll watch from the shore and if we see anything we'll advise them by torch'."

"But we didn't want any interference."

"I had explained that and I repeated it. They said they understood. Well, we drove about till it was dark, then we parked up a side road and went to Furnell's. We crept down to the river and hid behind shrubs near the boat-slip. I can tell you the time crawled. I got cramped and it wasn't long before I was wishing you and your problems far enough."

PART 2: THE BITERS BIT

French smiled. "It was in a good cause."

"That doesn't appeal so much if you're cold and cramped under a bush. But at least the night was fine. Though there was no moon, the stars were bright and we could see dimly. Well, we watched and about 1.00 a.m. it happened. Someone – we presumed Furnell – left the house and came softly down to the slip. He was carrying something and he put it down on the slip and went back to the house. Two or three minutes later he appeared again with a second load. He left it beside the first and went back again."

"Your chance?" put in French.

"It was and I took it. I slipped out and had a look at the packages. They were boxes about so big," Trent demonstrated with his hands, "and fairly heavy. I had scarcely got back to my place when the man came back with a third."

"Probably what Rawlins saw."

"I imagine so. Well, the man lifted the three into a dinghy and rowed out to the launch, which was only some fifty feet from the bank. Schneider had a torch with a tube projecting from the lens which screened the light from everywhere except directly ahead. He directed this to the River Service boat and morsed the news."

"There was no need for that surely," said French. "You had proved your case up to the hilt."

"So I thought. But let me tell you. For some time nothing happened and we settled down to await the return of Furnell, assuming it was he. Then suddenly there was a sharp but subdued voice from the launch. 'Well, sir, may I ask what you want?'

" 'Are you Captain Loxton?' a foreign voice said then in English.

"There was a reply: 'My name, sir, and may I ask again what you're doing here?'

"The foreign voice went on: 'I belong to the Swiss Customs and Excise River Service. That is my launch moored ahead of yours and some of my men are in a boat alongside. Please note that you are completely overpowered. I am about, Captain Loxton, to search your boat.'"

"But all that is just what we didn't want," French burst out angrily.

"It wasn't their fault; at least it wasn't done deliberately. You'll hear."

"It'll take some explaining," French's indignation grew impressive.

Trent made a pacific gesture. "You'll get it. Well, as you can imagine, I was amazed and couldn't understand what was happening. Then there was a call in German from the launch, 'Send down Fischer and Shaitegger and a couple of men to take charge,' and an answering hail from the Customs boat. Schneider turned to me.

"'I assure you this wasn't arranged,' he said. 'I warned them that the launch people weren't to know. I can't think what they've been up to.' Remembering what you had said, Joe, I was very much upset."

"You had cause to be."

"Yes, but it wasn't my fault. Then I consulted Schneider as to what we should do.

"He hailed the launch and asked them to send a boat for us. They said they would in a few moments. I could dimly make out the dark shape of a boat dropping down from the Customs launch. Then in a moment there were several people aboard the *Komforta*. They spoke in low tones and I could not hear what they said. Next I saw a boat moving towards the slip.

" 'Will you gentlemen come aboard?' invited the oarsman.

"I declare, Joe, in spite of all you've said, I was wishing for you as we crowded into the deck saloon. There was the whole thing laid out before our eyes. The place was full of long narrow tin boxes and each box contained watches. They had been brought aboard in Furnell's three cases. When we had time to go into it we found there were two-fifty boxes with eight watches in each. That meant two thousand watches in all. And can you guess where they were hidden?"

"Never mind the riddles," French grunted savagely. "Get on with the story."

"In the sundeck! There were slots in the thickness of the planking between the deck above and the ceiling below. The tin boxes were carried in the slots and the end sealed with a moveable moulding."

In spite of his annoyance French was so much interested that he insisted on a more detailed description with sketches.

"It's a brainy scheme all right," he admitted at last, "and only for Rawlins they might have got away with it for long enough. Then each trip was netting?"

"About three thousand pounds."

"Worth taking a risk for. But how did your friends come to give themselves away?"

"I asked that of course. They were very apologetic. It seemed that the chief, a man called Waldvogel, decided that he would drop down to the *Komforta* and try to see what was going on through a porthole. He intended to do this secretly. Well, they floated him down and then he found that all the portholes he could reach were blinded. He didn't want to give in and he thought he'd try the windows and portholes of the deck houses. The sides of the launch were too high for him to get on board silently, except at the companion way at the stern. Furnell's dinghy was tied up there, but they had plenty of room and he got silently on board and crept forward.

"Here the windows and portholes were also covered. He'd have been all right if he'd let it go at that, but he wasn't going to be beaten. He was that sort of man, you understand. He thought the others would be below and very gently he began to open the door of the deck saloon. This must have been seen, for Loxton slipped out of the door at the other side and came round and challenged him. Waldvogel then had to put the best face he could on it and we heard what happened."

"He should have done what he was asked," French growled savagely. "If the other members get away through it you'll have done me a bad turn."

"They won't get away. You listen."

"Go ahead."

"Well, a question arose then as to what was to be done. I assured Waldvogel that if the three men were arrested we'd apply for extradition. But he wouldn't move on his own responsibility and rang up his headquarters. There was a bit of a delay, then orders came through to arrest the men and impound the launch. So this was done. Before daybreak the men were in prison and the launch in a private dock, both near Basle."

French stared. "But they couldn't keep that dark."

"Not permanently, of course. But for a day or two they could and are doing. I needn't tell you that we then had a search: the men themselves, the launch and Furnell's

PART 2: THE BITERS BIT

house. By this time the police had found out that Furnell rented a small depot in Basle. One of his keys opened it and we searched it too. We didn't find much, but I think it'll be enough."

"What was it?" French's interest was making him forget his annoyance.

"First we learnt that at his depot Furnell was collecting watches. He bought them openly and some he sent openly to England. The scheme seemed to be good: if he was asked about his business he could prove these open dispatches."

"Yes, I expect that part of it'll be all right. Did you find out where he was sending them to?"

"Your finger on the spot as usual. Yes, it was to Baldwin's, a firm of watchmakers and distributors in Canterbury. That seemed to supply the missing link and it's why we're here."

French's main anxiety had now been dispelled. "At least it's a good tale," he admitted.

"I hope it's more than that. One other thing we found. In both Loxton's and Furnell's notebooks there were the same two numbers, one with an S before it and one with a C. They bothered me for a while, then I wondered could they be telephone numbers. The Canterbury address suggested what the C stood for. If so, where did the S come in?"

"You might have made a guess," said French. "What about Sandwich? That would be the exchange for the house belonging to Marsham's nephew, I imagine."

"As a matter of fact I did think of it. I rang up our people to find out, and I was right. The numbers were Baldwin's and Dolbey's."

"You seem to have made a job of it," French admitted with unwilling admiration.

Trent now moved uneasily and made deprecating gestures. "Now I'm coming to something that I don't like to tell you about. I did it more or less on the spur of the moment and I'm afraid now it wasn't very wise. But rightly or wrongly it's done and we'll have to act on it."

"You're not telling me you've spoilt a good piece of work?"

"No, I don't think so. But I'm not so sure of it as I was. I looked at it this way: we pretty well know Baldwin and Dolbey are in the thing, but are there more? It seemed to me that Dolbey would do the converse of Furnell and get the watches ashore. But could Baldwin distribute them without help? I thought it unlikely. At all events there was quite a chance that there were more in it."

"I don't see what you're getting at, but I'd be inclined to agree with you."

"Then I thought of something else or rather I had thought of it before this happened. What had Rawlins done to these people to make them get rid of him by murder? It seemed to me there could be only one answer. He was blackmailing them. Do you agree?"

French nodded. "Of course I agree. I never had any doubt about it."

"Very well, these two things suggested what I did and I hope you won't be very annoyed. I wrote to Baldwin threatening blackmail. I wrote to him because I thought that since he owned the works, he'd be the boss."

French stared speechlessly.

"I put it to myself like this," Trent went on hurriedly. "If there are more in it than two, we must have something to bring them all together. If they think they're confronted with more blackmail and perhaps another murder no one of them will act on his own responsibility. They'll talk it over. And they won't discuss it over the phone. They're

PART 2: THE BITERS BIT

bound to meet. Now my idea was that you and I and your friends should attend the meeting."

French struggled to control his feelings. "I'll have to hand it to you, Bob," he declared at length. "I wouldn't have done a thing like that if I'd lived to be a hundred. It's all wrong. It's so wrong I needn't begin to talk about it."

"But I've done it."

"But you've done it – and we must carry on."

"I thought you'd say so. Then here's a copy of the letter. I posted it in London about six this afternoon, so Baldwin should get it tomorrow when he reaches his works. He couldn't possibly have heard about the launch by then and it gives us time to make our plans."

French in a maze read the letter. "Who is this Hugh Kent or James Nolan to whom Baldwin is to write?"

"There's no such person as Hugh Kent. James Nolan is the name over a small stationer's shop. I rang up our Ramsgate representative and told him to phone me a likely address. Nolan of course knows nothing about it."

French chuckled grimly. "You've done a wholly irregular thing, but I'll give it to you that you've done it well. Now let's consider tomorrow. I propose," and he sketched out a rough programme. This they all agreed to without discussion.

"Next," French went on, "before we go any further we must approach the local super and take him into our confidence. After all we're hunting on his preserves."

Rollo glanced at his watch. "You mean now, sir?" he asked. "It's not eleven and the super should be available."

"Yes. I noticed the police station as we were driving in. It's quite close. We'd better walk round."

They went down together. "We're going to make a call on some friends," French explained to the night porter as they passed. "We'll probably be late back."

"That's be all right, sir. I'll be about."

At the police station French's name assured them of an obsequious welcome. Superintendent Richie had gone home, but the station sergeant rang him up and he replied that he would come down immediately. Fifteen minutes later he arrived.

"Very sorry to trouble you, particularly at this hour, Mr Richie," French explained, "but we're on a rather urgent case and we wanted to consult you about it and ask your kind help."

"Glad to do anything I can, Mr French."

"It's a compound affair," French went on: "smuggling in Swiss watches, which Mr Trent is looking after, and a murder which Rollo is handling. We believe the same parties are guilty of both. You'd better tell him your part of it, Bob."

Trent forthwith explained about the trips and his Swiss activities, Rollo recounted the affair of Rawlins, and French added the conclusions to which he had come. Superintendent Richie was impressed.

"And you propose to take them when they meet," he commented. "That letter of yours, Mr Trent, was a masterpiece, but I fear we poor hidebound police wouldn't have attempted it."

"I was speechless with horror when he told me of it," French agreed. "But we must act on it now."

Richie chuckled. "A virtue of necessity?" he queried. "Well, I'll certainly compound the felony with you, if that's what it is. What do you want me to do?"

"We called principally because we didn't want to be here without letting you know. But also we'd be grateful for your help. The first thing is: Could you have a man listen in to

PART 2: THE BITERS BIT

Baldwin's and Dolbey's telephones from when the post is delivered at the works in the morning?"

Richie took a note. "As you know, we can't demand that. But we're well in with the telephone people and they'll do it if we guarantee the authority later. Right, I'll send a girl to the exchange. What next?"

"Two men. One to assist Sergeant Trimble. Trimble with my car will shadow Dolbey – he knows him. If Dolbey meets Baldwin somewhere, as we expect he will, they're to shadow him to the meeting and then wait till they're called on. Rollo and I will shadow Baldwin, but another man with us who knows the area might be invaluable."

"Two local men. Right, I'll arrange that."

"Here, Joe, steady on," Trent put in. "You're leaving me out of this."

"I was going to ask you if you'd drive the car for Trimble? If Dolbey shows fight, Trimble and the constable should be free to deal with him. That way you'll be in at the finish."

"Anything else, Mr French?"

"I'm afraid there is, Mr Richie, and it won't be so easy because of the limited time available. We want to park in the street where we can watch the gate of Baldwin's works, and I hardly think we could do it in a private car. I wonder if you could borrow for us a light van? One of those green telephone vans would do – anything of that kind which could stand at the pavement without remark."

"Yes, I'll get it. Will you want overalls?"

"If your man would wear them and drive, Rollo and I could remain hidden inside."

"I'll see to it."

Next morning these arrangements were put into execution. Trimble and Trent went off with a constable who knew the area around the Stour. They parked not far from

ANYTHING TO DECLARE?

Dolbey's and Trimble and the constable took cover where they could watch the house. At the same time French and Rollo in an ordinary car had an engine breakdown in sight of the gate of Baldwin's house, which their constable-driver knew. This conveniently coming right at the moment when Baldwin appeared, they followed him to his works.

A plain clothes man immediately spoke to French's driver. "I'll watch till you come back," he said, and the car went on to police headquarters. In the yard was standing a Corporation Surveyor's Department light van. To this French and Rollo transferred and an overalled driver at once started. They parked in a side street facing the works, from which the gate was visible. The driver got out and began to walk about close by, French and Rollo remaining out of sight within. No one looked twice at the van.

Time now began to drag. They were not uncomfortable, having seats and being able to smoke if they wanted to, but French's mind was on the stretch. If their plan should miscarry it would be serious for him, particularly owing to the irregularity of Trent's stratagem. He would be glad when the episode was over.

They had been waiting for more than an hour when a man whom French recognized as a policeman in plain clothes strolled up and spoke to their driver. In his turn the driver passed the message to French. Baldwin had just rung up Dolbey saying: "A meeting this afternoon at usual time and place."

French was immensely relieved. The affair was going as it should. All they now had to do was to carry out their plan adequately and they would get their men.

But in spite of his easier mind, the hours seemed interminable. At lunch time they watched more intently, but Baldwin did not appear. The plain clothes man brought

PART 2: THE BITERS BIT

a parcel to their driver, and this to their great satisfaction proved to contain sandwiches and beer, sent with the Superintendent's compliments. Thus fortified, they settled down to another spell of waiting.

At half past five the employees began leaving the works gate. There were not many of them, some couple of dozen at the most. The driver started up his engine. Then at last Baldwin's car appeared. As it passed the end of their street they were able to see that it contained two men. The constable said that one was Baldwin, but he did not know the second.

The chase was an easy one. Baldwin was not driving quickly and they had no difficulty in keeping him in sight. The route lay out of the town, and as vehicles on the road grew fewer, they dropped further behind. At last after some ten minutes' run they reached a road junction.

"Grange Cross Roads," said the constable. "He's turning towards Whitstable."

They followed and almost at once passed the car containing Trent, Trimble and their constable, parked at the side of the road a little way behind another empty car. Looking back, French saw that they had started up and were following.

"That must be Dolbey's car and he must have walked on," French said, though doubtfully.

"That's he, sir, I bet," exclaimed Rollo.

They had just rounded a bend. In front Baldwin had stopped and a man was walking towards his car. In two seconds French had made up his mind.

"Pass him!" he directed his driver. "Step on it now! Don't let him get before us!"

They accelerated and passed Baldwin's car just after the man had got in and Baldwin was starting up. Trimble's car had fallen in behind Baldwin's.

"Now stop him!" went on French. "Get across his bows! Understand?"

The driver nodded. The road fortunately was clear. He swerved suddenly to the right and then round at full lock to the left. He was fairly across the road and he stopped some five feet from its left edge. This blocked as much of the road as possible. Baldwin could not pass to the left, but the road was wide and there was still sufficient space to the right. As Baldwin swung to the right, French's driver began to back in front of him. But this manoeuvre was not needed, for there was a sudden tearing noise. Trimble's car had accelerated and come up on the right, and as Baldwin pulled out the two vehicles ground into one another. But the impact was not severe. Both were going in the same direction at much the same speed, and beyond crushed wings little harm was done. Both came to a stand just short of French's car. Simultaneously French, Rollo, Trimble and the constables jumped out and Baldwin's car was surrounded.

"What's all this?" Baldwin cried sharply. "Who are you and what do you think you're doing?"

"We're police officers," French told him, "and we – Oh no, you don't!" and he flung open the door and seized Baldwin's hand as he was raising it to his mouth. At that same time the others closed in from both sides.

"A little pilule?" French went on, as he forced the hand open. "What's in it? Prussic acid? The game's up for all of you. We're taking you to headquarters on suspicion of having been concerned in the smuggling of Swiss watches."

The surprise and relief on the three suspects' faces was ample evidence to French that they had been expecting a very different accusation.

– 13 –

THE MISSING LINK

Until the men had been charged with the smuggling offence and lodged in the cells, French's mind was too much occupied to consider his next move. But that night as he settled down to think over what had happened, he grew more and more uneasy. Between them they had done a fine job for the Customs and Revenue and all six men were sure of a considerable stretch. But he was not interested in this matter, at least not professionally. His job was the conviction of the murderer of Rawlins, and for this he had no evidence that would stand for five minutes under a hostile counsel's cross examination.

An exhaustive search of the works and of the three men's houses made clear as day the entire working of the watch scheme, but did not produce a scintilla of evidence about the murder. There was of course the question of where Baldwin, Campion and Dolbey had been on the fatal Saturday night. As this could be ascertained better by local men, French enlisted Superintendent Richie's aid. At the same time he began in his slow painstaking way to work on such fresh information as had been obtained. First there were Baldwin's and Dolbey's cars. Could either of these be connected with that which had stood near Dr Marsham's on the night of the disappearance?

ANYTHING TO DECLARE?

Following a rather forlorn hope he borrowed a number of cars and lined them up at police headquarters, putting Baldwin's and Dolbey's among them. Trimble was sent to Folkestone for Albert Giles, the boy who had passed the parked car on the fateful night. He was told to walk down the line and point out, if he could, the vehicle he saw. This producing no result, French asked him to look again and rule out all those which it couldn't have been. Apparently Giles found this easier, for he quickly eliminated all but three. Baldwin's – though not Dolbey's – was among them, and the other two were of similar make. Useful confirmatory evidence if the case went to trial, but in itself no proof.

So far he had made little of it. French racked his brains to find some other line of approach. Presently it occurred to him that it was unlikely that on such an errand the car would have been driven under its own number-plates. He was therefore mildly thrilled when on re-examining Baldwin's car, he found that the fastenings of the plates showed recent movement. The joints had been wiped dry and blinded with dust, but a lens revealed the fresh oil below. Also the nuts unscrewed easily and the threads were oily.

Here might be a clue, though French was not hopeful of it. False plates could not be bought: only those bearing the correct number of the purchaser's car would be sold. Therefore false plates had to be made. It was practically certain also that no one embarking on a murder would employ an outsider to do the work. Therefore if there were false plates one of those three had made them.

French was not an expert, but he did not believe that any of the tools at the works could have been used. They were for more delicate operations. Nor had he found a workshop in either Baldwin's or Campion's houses. But Dolbey's

PART 2: THE BITERS BIT

outhouse seemed to contain everything needed for the job. Could he find out if Dolbey had done it?

Next morning with Rollo and Trimble he drove once more to the cottage on the Stour. In the workshop he noticed a partly used sheet of thin plate. Two rectangles had been cut from it, and as he measured the spaces he felt a tiny thrill. The missing pieces were one inch longer each way than Baldwin's plates. This would allow the necessary stiffening fold to be turned up all round.

"Keep that," he said to Rollo, "and mark on it where we got it. If we're lucky it'll be an exhibit."

Still searching about, French made his second find. He had noticed a number of pieces of what looked like white wall plaster. An examination showed that they were bits of the plastic sold for children to mould. He wondered what Dolbey had been doing with it. Continuing his search he unearthed a small moulded piece of the same material. It was about an inch long and half an inch wide with a triangular cross section, bevelled off at one end like a hipped roof. The surfaces were smooth except for the end opposite the bevel, which was rough and irregular. It was, he was positive, the end of a letter or number which had broken off.

"We're progressing," he said, as he handed the scrap to Rollo. "Take more care of it than if it was gold."

Letters and numbers, he saw, could easily be made of plastic and stuck on screws put in from the back of the plate. They would not last of course, but they would do the one journey for which they were required.

Before long he made a third discovery and one which removed any lingering doubt that he was on the right track. On the back of a board leaning against the wall he found some drops of what looked like white and black Chinese lacquers. There were tins of paint in the shop, but none of white or black. As it would be a coincidence if both these colours had run out at the same time, it looked as if the tins had been destroyed.

It was clear that plastic letters enamelled white fastened to a black plate and suitably dirtied would make excellent number-plates. French had no doubt that Dolbey had made them. But still he could not prove it. Nor did a further search of the premises reveal anything fresh.

"I think," French said when this was complete, "we'll get the local men to start an inquiry as to whether Dolbey or those others were seen anywhere about that night. If Dolbey was one of the men with the car at Folkestone, as is likely because he knew the place, he might have been noticed going or returning."

"That would be useful, sir."

"Yes, we'll go to the local station and start the thing."

The sergeant was impressed when he learnt the identity of his visitors. He said none of his men had made any report on that night, but he would see them and find out if they could help. "There was something, I think it was that night, sir," he went on. "If you'll excuse me I'll look it up." He turned over the pages of a book. "Yes, it was that night. It was one of the coastguards. He didn't make a formal report, but just mentioned the thing when he was talking."

"What was that, Sergeant?"

"It was about two in the morning and he was patrolling on the shore along Pegwell Bay when he saw a light appear suddenly off the mouth of the river. A moment later a motor started up. It sounded to him like an outboard motor, but of course he couldn't be sure. The boat or whatever it was went on towards the sea and he lost sight of it."

"That might be useful enough."

PART 2: THE BITERS BIT

"There's more than that, sir. Some three quarters of an hour later he heard it again, far away. He watched and soon he saw the light. It came in from the sea and went towards the river. He waited to find out if it would go up, but when it came to where he had seen it first, the motor stopped and the light went out."

"That's all very interesting. How far from Dolbey's cottage did this take place?"

The sergeant shook his head. "I'm afraid I couldn't say that, sir, but if you have a few minutes I can fetch the coastguard."

"We'll go and see him. Get into the car with us, Sergeant."

The coastguard was asleep after a night on duty, but he quickly came down. French put his question.

The man couldn't say exactly, but he estimated that the light had gone out and reappeared about a mile below Dolbey's. After the motor stopped he had listened for oars, but had not heard them. There was a certain amount of noise from the slight wind and the splash of the waves. He didn't think even if there had been rowing that he could have heard it.

"Come back with us to Mr Dolbey's cottage," French directed. When they reached it he went on, "Look at the stern of the boat and see if you can find any traces of where an outboard motor has been fixed."

There were, it appeared, faint marks on the wood and the coastguard was sure that they had been caused in this way. It was suggestive news and the fact that there was no such motor on the premises made it more interesting still.

"Well, Rollo," French said when the others had gone, "what do you make of all that?"

"Hard to believe Dolbey's boat wasn't out, sir."

"And what for?"

"I don't think there can be much doubt about that. I suggest they were getting rid of the body."

At this Trimble nodded emphatically. "He would drop the motor overboard, sir," he suggested, "so that it couldn't be found at his place."

This was what French also believed, so all were of one mind. The next step was obvious. Inquiries were made from suppliers of outboard motors in London and the south-east as to applications received for a motor suitable for Dolbey's boat. Of the replies one immediately attracted French's attention both because of its location and its date. It was from a small shop in Margate and the purchase was made on the day before the murder. French thought that if Rawlins had shown his hand that week, as seemed likely, the decision to murder him could only have been taken a day or two before the deed. In this case there would not have been time to go further afield for the purchase.

A short run brought the three men to Margate. The manager of the shop proved a pleasant efficient-looking man named Orwell.

"Oh yes," he replied to French's question, "the constable was making inquiries about that. Is it what you want?"

"We think so," said French. "Please let us have particulars."

It was, Mr Orwell told them, about ten in the morning when a middle-aged man called and asked about small sized outboard motors. The two assistants were engaged and Orwell dealt with the business himself. The man had given the size of his boat and had looked at two or three motors. He had selected one, paid the money in notes, carried the motor out to his car and driven off. There was nothing remarkable about the transaction.

PART 2: THE BITERS BIT

French thanked him. "Now, Mr Orwell, there are two things we want you to do. This is a serious case, a murder, and your help has become essential."

"Of course I'll do anything I can," Orwell returned, adding with a smile: "No option, have I?"

French smiled also. "We'll be grateful for your help at all events. First, we ask the loan of a similar motor to check it against marks on the stern of a boat."

"That's easy. I can let you have it now."

"Good. I'm afraid the second thing isn't so easy. We want you to run over to Canterbury and see if you can identify the purchaser in a parade."

"That's an unpleasant duty, but I see of course that it must be done."

In both these matters French felt that at last they were making progress. When they tried the motor they found that it registered exactly with the marks, and at the parade Orwell unhesitatingly picked out Campion.

French now turned to his next item. He wished to check the results of the local men who had been put on to find out where the three suspects had been on the fatal Saturday evening. He therefore called for their reports. These were clear and comprehensive.

Since Dolbey lived alone his movements had not been ascertained, but it had been learnt that Baldwin and Campion had been from home during the critical hours. They had told their households that they were going to a business dinner in London, and as they could not get home they would stay overnight. Asked would they care to state where the dinner was held and where they had slept, they at first refused, then said that this was only a tale for their wives and that they had spent the night at Baldwin's works. They were trying to think out a way of getting the watches ashore before the launch reached the Stour. They felt it was desirable that Dolbey should demonstrate that nothing secret went on during the vessel's visit by inviting a friend to stay with him for the week. French did not believe a word of the story, but he saw how a skilful counsel could use it for the defence.

In spite of this it was highly satisfactory to know that these two had been from home at the time of the murder. The evidence was accumulating nicely. A few more facts and they would have their case.

He was considering whether he could now return to London when he was called to the telephone. It was Superintendent Rider.

"We've just had a call from Dr Marsham. He sounded fairly het up. He says he's learnt something that we should know and he wanted to see me. I told him you were the man for it. What do you say? Will you go?"

"Will I not?" French retorted. "What do you take me for? That doctor's no fool, and if he says he's got something, he certainly has."

"Right, I'll phone him that you'll be there in – ?"

"Couple of hours."

Just two hours later French and Trimble were shown into the doctor's study. Marsham seemed agitated and feeble and somehow both excited and depressed. He greeted them shortly.

"I've had some terrible news, gentlemen. It has shaken me badly. I longed to keep it to myself, but I saw that I could not do so. Justice must be done." He lowered his head and seemed overcome.

"I'm sorry, sir," French answered smoothly, "that you have been distressed. But of course you are right. In vital matters information cannot be held back. I can assure you

PART 2: THE BITERS BIT

that we shall not use anything you may say unless it is absolutely necessary."

"This will be necessary. It was Miss Kelso. Something she saw. She will tell you herself." He rang and asked for Nancy.

To deal with persons in mental anguish was nothing new for French, but he was sorry when he noted Nancy's pallor, her swollen eyes and despairing expression.

"Come and sit down, my dear," Marsham greeted her. "Just tell Mr French what you saw. It won't take long."

French remembered that he had been puzzled by her manner on his first call, insomuch that he had wondered if she was keeping something back. But nothing of this showed in his bearing. He greeted her pleasantly and told her that she was to take her time and not allow herself to be worried. She looked at him gratefully and with apparent surprise that a police officer could be so kind. Then she began her story.

"It was on that Saturday night, that awful Saturday. It was a little after nine, five or ten minutes, I should think. The nine o'clock News had begun and I don't think it was finished."

"Near enough, madam."

"I was on the way up to my room when I heard soft steps in the back passage. I thought Rawlins had returned and I moved a step or two across so that I could see down the passage. I intended to wish him good evening and to show some interest in his holiday. But it wasn't Rawlins." She stopped as if she found it too painful to proceed.

"It was Mr Dolbey, madam?" French suggested quietly.

"Oh!" she cried, "then you know! Then I needn't have had all this" – she paused for a word – "this hesitation about telling you!"

"I did not know, Miss Kelso, but I guessed. Go on, please, with your story."

"Well, it was as you say. It was Valentine, though he had tried to disguise himself. I was just going to call out, 'Hullo, Val! What brings you here?' when I noticed his face. Mr French, it was the face of – of a devil. I'm sorry, doctor, to have to say it," she turned to Marsham, "but nothing else would describe it."

"My poor girl," Marsham said with sympathy, "of course you must describe things as you saw them."

She was obviously fighting to hold back her tears. "You're so good," she muttered, then went on to French. "I was scared stiff and remained silent. He didn't see me. He stopped at Rawlins' door and opened it gently. He went in and I heard the soft click of its being locked behind him."

"What did you do then?"

"I didn't know what to do. I thought, it's no business of mine, but I knew from his face that something must be badly amiss and I felt that I must watch what happened."

"You were very right, madam."

"I don't know, but that's what I did. I waited in my room with the door open and the light out for perhaps quarter of an hour. Then faintly I heard the door being unlocked and closed again. I peeped out and saw Val creeping to the back stairs. He went down. I thought to myself that if he wished to remain unseen he could not go out through the kitchen, as cook was there. So I sat down at the head of the stairs from where you could see the front hall and watched."

"I certainly congratulate you on your action," French put in.

"As I got there you, doctor, came out of the sitting-room and went into your bedroom. As soon as you were inside I saw Val. He tiptoed across the hall to the front door. But

PART 2: THE BITERS BIT

just as he got to it Julia – that is, Miss Parratt – came out of the doctor's bedroom. Val flattened himself against the wall and she didn't see him. But she was coming upstairs, so I slipped back into my room. When I was able to look out again Val had gone."

When she ceased speaking there was silence for a few moments. Then French broke it.

"I'm very grateful for your statement, Miss Kelso. I had guessed that something like that had happened, though I wasn't sure. But naturally I must ask why you didn't report this at the time?"

She wrung her hands. "I know. I see now I should have done so. But at first it didn't seem important. I felt sure that he and Rawlins were up to something bad, but I didn't see that it was my business. In fact – "

"In fact, that wasn't the reason at all," Marsham broke in. "She kept it back because of me."

"Because of you, sir?"

"Valentine is my nephew and I am fond of him. She thought it would pain me to know."

"I'm afraid pain can't be avoided in these cases."

The doctor sighed. "No, Mr French, wrongdoing brings its own reward. But that isn't the point. We all noticed from Miss Kelso's manner that something was distressing her, but she wouldn't tell us what. Then – "

"It was when we learnt that Val had been arrested," Nancy interrupted. "There was the terrible suggestion in the paper that Rawlins had been murdered. I couldn't – "

"We didn't let her keep silence. It was evident that she was breaking her heart over something and I practically forced her to tell me. It was a blow," the doctor's voice all but broke, "I don't pretend it wasn't a blow. But of course there was only one thing to be done. I rang up Mr Rider."

"It was hard, sir, for you, but obviously your decision was right. We were practically satisfied that Mr Dolbey and his associates had driven here to your road on Saturday evening. They interrupted Rawlins on his way back and took him away in the car."

"Dreadful!"

"We felt sure Mr Dolbey had been in the house. There was the matter of Rawlins' passport. It was probably in his room, as it was unlikely he had taken it to Ramsgate. But if it were found there it would give the Brazil story away. They had to get it and obviously Mr Dolbey was the man to do it. So, Miss Kelso, you only confirmed what we already knew."

"I'm glad – I'm glad of that."

Though French really did feel for these nice people, he could not but be profoundly satisfied with their information. Proof – obvious proof that a jury would accept – he now had against Campion and Dolbey. There was a weight of evidence against Baldwin, but unhappily nothing actually connecting him with the crime. How to get such further evidence French did not know. He pondered over it doubtfully, then decided that the time had come for a conference.

– 14 –

THE CROWNING ITEM

It was in the early afternoon that French, Rider, Rollo and Trimble sat down in the super's room to take stock of the position and consider future action. For Rider's benefit French reviewed the evidence which had been obtained. "You see," he explained, "we've now got satisfactory proof against Dolbey and Campion. Dolbey we could have got through the making of the number-plates, but that is unnecessary since we can prove he was in Rawlins' room just after the man's disappearance. Miss Kelso's story would go down better with a jury and we'll concentrate on it. Campion we have through the purchase of the outboard motor, and the facts that it is no longer to be found and that its marks shown on Dolbey's boat indicate how it was used. But we've nothing directly against Baldwin."

"The general circumstances, sir, his meeting with the others and his attempt to commit suicide?" Rollo queried.

"Yes, quite so," French agreed. "They make his guilt extremely likely and they convince me. But would they convince a jury?"

"I should have thought so, sir."

"You may be right and if we can't do better we'll have to depend on them. All the same, if we could get direct proof I'd much prefer it. What do you say, Mr Rider?"

Rider nodded. "I agree with all you've said. I think even if you can't get more evidence you're pretty safe. I've known convictions to be obtained with less. But that's assuming that the one outstanding defect in the evidence is overcome."

"You mean the absence of a body?"

"Yes."

"I need scarcely say that it's been continuously in my mind," French answered. "Of course a conviction of murder has been obtained before now without one, and I suppose it could be again. But I agree that for a satisfactory case Rawlins' body must be produced."

"If it's at the bottom of the sea, sir, as we believe," put in Rollo, "there doesn't seem to be much chance of getting hold of it."

"No, it's not a promising outlook. And yet I'm not certain that it's hopeless. I've been puzzling over it and I think there's one possibility."

"You do?" said Rider. "Well, that interests me. I should have thought it quite out of the question."

"I admit it's doubtful. The attempt would be expensive and it mightn't succeed, so Sir Mortimer mightn't stand for it."

"I'd hate to put ideas into your head," Rider said dryly, "but it occurs to me your AC needn't be asked. As a matter of fact, wouldn't it be our charge?"

French stared at him, then gave a hoot of laughter. "I believe I'm going dotty," he declared. "I was thinking so much about how the thing might be done that I overlooked that essential. Right, that's fine! Now the question is, would you foot the bill?"

Rider laughed in his turn. "A blank cheque? You could hardly expect the CC to stand for that. He's fond of the

PART 2: THE BITERS BIT

Yard, but not to that extent. He'd want some kind of an estimate."

"I suppose he would. But speaking seriously, Super, I'd naturally put the whole thing before you and Major Hope. I'd of course get the best possible estimate. But I'd say straight out that there was only a fifty-fifty chance of success."

Rider considered this. "If the cost wasn't too staggering he'll probably be on for it. He was delighted to hear of the arrests and I know he'll be very much upset if there are no convictions."

"I've had this in my mind for some time," French resumed, "but there hasn't been time to follow it up. I'd like to do so now, so I suggest we have a meeting with your CC. Then I'll put all my cards on the table."

"I'll ring him up now," Rider agreed. He was occupied for some time with the telephone, calling various places. Then he turned back to French.

"I've traced him to Dover. He'll be done there in half an hour and he'll come straight over. It's," he glanced up at the clock, "just four. I suggest a cup of tea would fill the time adequately."

To this there was no dissenting voice and they went out to a nearby café. There French described his scheme. The others were impressed and Rider said he was sure the CC would fall for it.

At the meeting Major Hope was complimentary both about what had been done and what was now proposed. For the latter professional marine help would be required, and he and Rider agreed that this could best be provided by a Dover salvage firm. Rider then and there rang these people up and obtained a rough estimate of the cost. The CC appeared to think the amount not unreasonable. "If that covers it," he said, "I think we can stand for it. What do you say, Mr Rider?"

"I agree with you, sir. Those three men are as guilty as sin and I shouldn't like to see them getting off on a legal quibble. Though what we've learnt is due to Mr French's work, the credit of this force is also at stake."

"Of course. Well, I agree it's worth trying. Go ahead, Mr French. You have our money and our good wishes behind you." On this happy note the proceedings terminated.

"Now," said French to Rollo and Trimble, "Sandwich seems to be the idea. We'll drive over at once, stay the night, and when we've got our information tomorrow, drop in on the salvage people at Dover. But before we go I want to phone the Yard for an Ordnance map. It can be sent to Sandwich."

They carried out their plan. After dinner French relaxed sufficiently to accompany the others to a Western film, the only attraction which Sandwich seemed to offer. Though extraordinarily dull, it was at least a change of thought.

Next morning they began operations by calling at the police station for the map, which had been sent from town on the previous evening. It was of six inches to the mile scale, covering the mouth of the Stour and showing Dolbey's cottage and part of Pegwell Bay. "Now for our friend the coastguard," said French and Rollo started up once more.

They were lucky in the weather. The morning had been misty, but now the sun had broken through and the air was clearing quickly. There was a gentle breeze from the west, but not enough to roughen the water.

When they arrived the coastguard was finishing breakfast after a night out. French apologized for keeping him from his bed.

PART 2: THE BITERS BIT

"That's all right, sir," the man returned. "I'm only too glad if I can be of use."

"Your information may be important," French told him, "so we'll ask you for an hour of your time. It's about that night when you saw the boat. We want to know everything you can tell us about it."

"Yes, sir?"

"I have to explain that you may be called on to give evidence in court, so you must be careful that you can stand over everything you say."

"Yes, sir, I'll be careful."

"Then just step into the car and take us to where you were when you saw the light spring up."

They turned into the main Ramsgate road along Pegwell Bay. At a certain point the coastguard halted. "It was here, sir. I remember clearly. I was just opposite that hut."

"And in what direction was the boat?"

The coastguard swung round, then pointed out across the water. "Just there, sir. There was a light on the other side and I knew it was from that cottage, for the wife's ill and they have a light all night. The boat's light was nearly in line with it, actually about two degrees to port."

French carefully marked the points on his map. "That's where you saw the light start up. Now let's go to where you were when it went out."

"It wasn't very far away, sir, not more than a couple of hundred yards nearer Ramsgate. I'd been to the end of my beat and was returning."

"Let's go to it all the same."

They walked the distance indicated. Once again the coastguard gave the direction and French noted it on his map.

"Thank you. Now about times. Can we get them more accurately? In your report to the police you said that about three quarters of an hour elapsed between the light coming on and going off. Can you do better than that?"

As the affair was unusual and a trifle suspicious, the coastguard had noted everything he could about it. He drew a notebook from his pocket and turned over the leaves. "I have the actual times here," he answered. "The light appeared at two and it went out again at two forty-eight."

"That's excellent. Now one more matter and I've finished. The tide? Can you tell me how it was running that night?"

The coastguard drew a small printed table from his pocket. He consulted it, then made some calculations. "High water was at twelve-thirty that night, sir. It was within four days of springs. During the boat's journey the ebb would be running fairly strongly."

"And high water tonight?"

"Very nearly the same. About midnight."

"And the run?"

"Much the same, but a little stronger. Two days to top springs instead of four."

"Well," said French, "we're much obliged to you. Now I take it you're prepared to repeat all that in the witness box?"

"Oh yes, sir. Certainly."

"Then come back to the car and we'll run you home."

"A marvellous bit of luck!" French declared when they had left the cottage. "If that man had been on some other beat or hadn't been so observant we mightn't have got the information, and then my scheme would have been a wash-out."

PART 2: THE BITERS BIT

"Lucky indeed, sir. Where do we head now?"

"You ought to be running this show, Rollo, not I. Go to that outboard motor shop in Margate. What was the manager's name? Orwell, wasn't it?"

"That's right, sir."

"Tell me, can either of you work an outboard motor, I mean, to get the best out of it?"

"I can, sir," Trimble answered. "I've done quite a lot in boats at Folkestone at one time or another."

"Well, we'll employ you as our engineer."

It was getting on to lunch time when they reached Margate, but Orwell had not gone out.

"We want a further favour from you, Mr Orwell," French explained. "We want to hire a similar outboard motor to that purchased by our suspect, Campion. But this time we want to use it. We want to know at what speed it will drive our boat."

Mr Orwell smiled as he shook his head. "Well, gentlemen, I'm afraid we don't hire out our motors; if we did we could scarcely sell them as new. But I'll tell you what I can do. I can sell you a motor and when you've finished with it I can buy it back as second-hand. It would come to much the same thing to you, for your loss on the transaction would be little more than the amount you'd pay for hire."

French smiled in his turn. "The bookkeeping doesn't interest us. If we get the motor for a period we're prepared to pay what's right. But there's a more important point. How nearly have similar motors the same horsepower?"

"Unless something's wrong the performance should be practically equal."

"Good enough. Then can we have one similar to that sold to Campion?"

ANYTHING TO DECLARE?

This was quickly loaded up with the necessary oil and petrol. After a snack lunch the three officers were again on the road. It did not take them long to reach the cottage. Dolbey's dinghy had been lifted into his garage, but they soon carried it to the water and with oars, the outboard motor and French's map they got aboard.

"Full speed ahead," French adjured Trimble, continuing: "On that Saturday night when those three went down the river the tide was running out. It's doing so again at present. Now, Rollo, while Trimble minds his engine I want you to time our speed, by which I mean the time it takes us to go from when I tell you to start to when I tell you to stop. You follow?"

"Yes, sir."

"We'll both do it and compare results. Get ready, for we're coming to the place."

They had passed out of the river and entered on Pegwell Bay when French, who had been taking a bearing between two outstanding objects on shore, called "Start!" Both men read their watches while French marked his bearing points on the map.

"I'm keeping to the fairway," Trimble put in. "That right, sir?"

"Yes, that's right."

French was urgently searching for another bearing and now he found one. "Stop!" he called. "What do you make that, Rollo?"

"Ten minutes forty seconds."

"I got that too. Since we agree we may take it as correct. Half a moment till I get that bearing on the map." He bent over it.

"Now, Trimble, I want to do the same thing in the opposite direction. Turn, will you, and we'll run back."

PART 2: THE BITERS BIT

Again they timed their progress. Again both agreed. They made it 17 minutes 20 seconds.

"Good," French approved. "That finishes us. Back to the hotel as quick as we can."

They replaced the dinghy in Dolbey's garage and drove to Sandwich. French was impatient to get at his calculations, but it was so nearly supper time that he had to wait till the meal was over. Then, commandeering one of the tables in the dining-room, he spread his map on it and began. Rollo and Trimble watched with keen interest.

"The first thing," began French, "is to get the coastguard's lines on the map. Now here," he pointed, "is the hut he stood beside and here is the house with the light in the window."

As he spoke French drew a line across the Bay joining the points. "That's got it," he resumed. "Now it was on that line and presumably in the fairway, say there," and he marked a point, "that the boat was when the light went on and the motor started up. You both agree?"

Both agreed with fervour. They were eagerly following his work.

"Next one," went on French, and in the same careful way the coastguard's second line was ruled. "That's where the light went out. You see, the two points are so close to one another that we may take them as one."

"It's what the coastguard reported, sir."

"Yes, he wasn't far wrong." French then ruled in the other two lines, those which he had himself chosen and between which they had timed the runs of the dinghy. In each case he marked the centre of the fairway, which was about where the boat had passed.

"All that's preliminary," he explained, "now we can get on to the real thing." He took the rule and measured between the last pair of lines. "Five and a quarter inches. That's the length on the map of our speed trial: a bit less than a mile. Now look up our times: 10 minutes 40 seconds down and 17 minutes 20 seconds up. Let's add those together. I make it 28 minutes."

They all made it 28 minutes.

"Very well," French continued, "see what that gives us. It took us 28 minutes to go up and down a length represented by 5¼ inches on the map. That right?"

Again both agreed.

"Consider now Dolbey's boat on the Saturday night. The light went on at 2.00 and went off again at 2.48. That's to say it was shining for 48 minutes?"

"Right, sir."

"During that 48 minutes the boat went from the point where the light came on down towards the sea and back again. Now, Rollo, if the same boat with a similar engine went 5¼ inches in 28 minutes, how many inches would it go in 48 minutes?"

"I begin to get it, sir," Rollo answered with excitement. For a moment he calculated, then gave his result. "Just 9 inches."

"That's what I make it," French agreed. "Now we'll transfer that to the map." Again he scaled and made a dot, around which he put a small circle. "There," he went on, pointing dramatically to his dot, "or thereabouts, unless I'm greatly mistaken, lies the body of Joseph Rawlins!"

Rollo and Trimble were enthusiastic, but French slightly damped their ardour by his further remarks. "The body must be somewhere about that distance from where the light vanished and reappeared, but we don't know how far it may be sideways from our line. We've taken the normal course out into the bay, but Dolbey may have kept more

PART 2: THE BITERS BIT

either to right or left. However, the body must be on the arc of a circle and the area of search will be small."

"Is there no fear, sir, that currents may have carried the body further off?" Trimble asked.

"Well, what do you think? They had to weight the body to make certain it wouldn't float and perhaps be picked up. I should imagine that they weighted it so heavily that it wouldn't move."

"I'm sure you're right, sir."

"One more point and we're done for tonight," French went on. "I'd like if possible to get cross bearings for that body area. Without them we'd never identify the place." He pored over the map. "That might do for one," he said presently. "If we can identify those two houses on the ground, a line joining them goes near enough through our point."

"We should be able to find the houses."

"Yes, I think so. Now something more or less at right angles to that. There we are, I think. Those two sheds." He pointed. "Well, thanks to our coastguard that's worked out better than we could have hoped."

The next morning the affair was carried a step further.

They drove to Dover to the office of the salvage firm, Messrs Jordan & Son. Mr Jordan, the senior partner, saw them at once. French explained the position and produced his map.

"We have reason to believe that the body must be in or near the area marked by this circle. And here, you see, we've indicated what may prove to be useful cross bearings. If we're right, sir, what do you think of the chances of getting the body?"

"If you're right, Mr French, almost a dead cert. We could do it with divers, but I have two very expert frogmen, and over a limited area like that and in comparatively shallow water, they could work admirably."

"I'm much relieved to hear you say so. As you know, our local Chief Constable has agreed to foot the bill. I should like to ask you when you can make the attempt?"

The senior partner considered. "I know Major Hope well and I should like to oblige him, and you also, Mr French. The frogmen are not particularly busy today and I think I could let them go at once. I usually like to start this kind of work in the morning, but seeing there's a hurry, our launch could be at the place by one o'clock. They'd have the afternoon to make a trial."

"Nothing could be better, sir. I'm immensely obliged."

On leaving the office French drove to a marine store and bought a small marker buoy, an anchor and a few fathoms of light rope. "We'll go out to that place when we get back," he decided, "and try and mark our point. If we can do so it'll save time when the others come. So now to Dolbey's cottage."

Again they got out the dinghy and outboard motor, and having loaded up their purchases, they pushed off. Once more they were lucky in the day. It was mild for late September. The sun was bright, the sky cloudless, and in the clear atmosphere everything was looking its best. More important still, the water was calm and reasonably warm. They soon passed out into Pegwell Bay. French began trying to identify the buildings ashore with those on his map.

"There we are," he said presently, pointing. "It's the right-hand house of those three, and we have to get it in line with that white one further back. Easy now, Trimble. I ring you 'Slow Ahead'. Rollo, get ready to drop that anchor."

For some time they manoeuvred till at last both the bearings registered. Then French called, "Let go!" and the

PART 2: THE BITERS BIT

little anchor went over with a splash. About half the line ran out after it.

"Rollo, make fast to the marker buoy and throw it over."

There was no anchor in the dinghy, so Trimble kept the motor running slowly, and when they drifted with the tide, used it to return to the buoy.

"We found that place more easily than I expected," French remarked. "Our friends are not likely to be here for at least an hour, so I suggest we investigate that parcel which Rollo has made up."

It was French's foresight which in Dover had suggested the parcel. Now they opened it and found three bottles of beer and a huge packet of sandwiches. Dealing with these kept them contentedly occupied for some time.

It was nearer two hours than one when Trimble gave a shout. "There, sir," he pointed. "If that's not the salvage launch I'll eat my hat."

Coming up from the south was a small craft. It was heading almost straight for them, keeping close inshore and far from the shipping lane to the east.

"It's either for us or it's going up the river," French agreed.

It drew quickly nearer and presently Trimble was able definitely to identify it. French stood up and waved, pointing to the buoy. The man at the wheel waved back. The launch's speed slackened, she floated slowly to the buoy and dropped anchor. Trimble brought the dinghy alongside.

"We've dropped the buoy from cross bearings taken from our map," French explained to the helmsman, who turned out also to be the master. "This is where we think the body may be, but you will understand that our estimate can't be dead accurate, and your people may have to cover a pretty wide area."

"I understand that all right," returned the master, "but you've speeded up the work by what you've done. Now the launch marks your point sufficiently well. I suggest you pick up your marker so as to have it to drop if we find anything."

"We'll do so," French returned.

"Then I think the best plan would be for the launch to remain here at anchor, while you take the dinghy round it in a gradually increasing spiral. In this shallow water the men could see the dinghy from below."

"Right. Can you fix that, Trimble?"

"Oh yes, sir."

The three police officers were greatly interested in what followed. The frogmen quickly undressed, put the rubber attachments on their feet, and had their breathing apparatus fixed on their backs and tested. Then both plunged in. Trimble cast off from the launch and began spiralling. This went on for some little time and then one man after the other broke surface and swam to the launch.

"They're having a bit of a rest," called the master. "They'll go down again presently."

French waved back and Trimble busied himself in keeping the dinghy in the same position. The tide had been against them when they came downstream, but now the hour of high water had passed and the ebb was beginning. The run was not strong enough to inconvenience the frogmen and they soon re-entered the water, swam to the dinghy, and there dived. Trimble resumed his spiral, while all waited anxiously for further manifestations.

Again the men came up for a spell, and when they went down all once again watched the surface, hoping against hope for success.

PART 2: THE BITERS BIT

Then suddenly it happened. One of the men appeared. He signed that he had found something and pointed downwards. Trimble immediately brought the dinghy to the place and Rollo threw out the anchor, rope and marker buoy. The frogman went down again, but immediately reappeared, nodding. French presumed they had marked correctly. While the launch was moving slowly to the place and anchoring, both frogmen had another rest. One of them could be seen deep in discussion with the master. Then from a small derrick the launch let down a light rope with a hook at the end. The frogman went in again beside the rope. It shook about in the water and the frogman reappeared.

"There's a chain round the remains, Mr French," the master called. "They've put the hook under the chain, so we'll have it up in a moment. You'd better come aboard, I think. This is more in your line than ours."

The body, when at last it lay on the deck, was a terrible sight. Over three weeks' immersion and the attacks of fish had left only a ghastly semblance of what had once been Rawlins. French was accustomed to such dreadful appearances, but even he found it all he could do to carry on.

"For heaven's sake put a flag or something over it," he urged. The master, himself much moved, hurried to do so. An ensign was produced, laid down, and weighted all round to keep it in place. Even then all avoided that part of the deck. With relief French turned to the master.

"Could your men do one more dive?"

"Yes, if it's not too long."

"Then follow us over here."

French returned to the launch and steered to the point at which the light had gone out and reappeared. "It's not a body this time," he told the master, "but an outboard motor. We reckon it must be close to this point."

Once again the men went down and once again French's forecast was justified. In less than fifteen minutes the motor was found and lifted aboard.

"Can you take me to Folkestone?" French called to the master. "The inquiry's being run from there and it would be convenient."

"Certainly. You're paying for the boat and we'll take you to Kamchatka if you want to go."

French forced a smile and called Rollo. "You and Trimble go back with the dinghy to Dolbey's, then run to Folkestone in the car. At the first call box ring up Superintendent Rider. Tell him what's happened and say we'll want a stretcher and conveyance to meet us. If you're there before us you can help."

In spite of their terrible passenger French enjoyed the run down the coast. The afternoon had remained warm and sunny, and the master turned out to be a pleasant fellow, full of sound sense and interesting anecdotes. As they approached the South Foreland they entered the shipping lane and French, who was fond of the sea and ships, was thrilled by the number and variety of the vessels passing up and down the Straits. Then Dover appeared, drew abeam, dropped astern and was lost to view. Shortly afterwards they swung round to starboard and entered Folkestone Harbour.

Rollo and Trimble had not yet arrived, but they had obviously sent their message, for on the wharf were waiting two constables with a stretcher and covered van. As the launch moored they came aboard, the body was lifted on to the stretcher and with the outboard motor was carried to the van. Ten minutes later both had been placed in the

PART 2: THE BITERS BIT

station mortuary and French was being congratulated by Superintendent Rider.

"It was a piece of luck," French assured him. "If that coastguard hadn't been there and taken those notes we should have been sunk. We couldn't have searched the whole of Pegwell Bay."

"All's well that ends well, which is trite, but I've found it true," Rider returned. "I suppose you've now got your case?"

"Yes, certainly against Campion and Dolbey. I'm still not so sure about Baldwin. But we'll try again."

"You'll try till you get it. I know you by this time. What's your next move?"

"I shall want the clothes and the contents of the pockets. It occurs to me that that housemaid, Edith Jones, should be able to identify them. The medical evidence as to the date of death would also be helpful."

"We've rung up Dr Carling. He should be here any time. Would you like me to send out for Edith Jones?"

"No need to trouble you, Super. Rollo and Trimble are on their way and they can go."

"As you wish."

When the doctor arrived French went with him to the mortuary. While not committing himself to a day, Carling put the date of death some three or four weeks earlier. Actually it was twenty-five days since the fatal Saturday night. So this fitted.

There followed the appalling job of stripping the clothes off the remains. After he had emptied the pockets, French had everything washed. While this was taking place Rollo and Trimble turned up and were at once sent off for Edith Jones. Twenty minutes later she was at the station. French greeted her sympathetically.

ANYTHING TO DECLARE?

"I'm afraid what we have to ask you to do, Miss Jones, is rather horrible, but there's nothing else for it. I take it you know what happened?"

"Yes, sir. Mr Rollo told me." Edith looked frightened and unhappy.

"Well, it won't take you long. Just have a look at these clothes and objects from the pockets and see if you can identify them. Don't do so unless you're quite sure, for I'm afraid you may have to give evidence about it in court."

It proved a trying experience for all concerned, but at least it was conclusive. Edith unhesitatingly identified both clothes and certain objects from the pockets.

The evidence from the outboard motor was equally conclusive. Its serial number enabled Orwell to state positively that it was that motor and no other which he had sold to Campion.

French felt that he had now obtained all the evidence necessary for a conviction, and it was only his training in thoroughness that prompted him to seek for more. But when he considered the length of heavy chain which had been round the body, he thought it might prove fruitful. It was unlikely that any of the three had such a chain in his possession, and if it had been at Baldwin's works he could scarcely have taken it lest it should be missed. Probably therefore, like the outboard motor, it had been bought for the occasion. It might be worth while trying to trace the purchase.

Then followed another piece of routine work. Since Campion had bought the motor in Margate, it looked as if he had not had time to go further afield. Perhaps the same condition obtained in the case of the chain? At all events they would begin with nearby towns.

PART 2: THE BITERS BIT

In a very short time French's reasoning was justified. The purchase had been made in Margate. The shop assistant who had sold it could swear to the type, and he turned up notes of the weight and length. French arranged for the identity parade usual in such circumstances and then with a thrill he reaped his reward. The assistant identified Baldwin as the purchaser.

With immense relief French realized that this discovery put the coping stone on his edifice of proof. Now he had direct evidence, against all three men. Now he could produce the body. His case was complete.

As he helped Rollo to get the records in order for submission to the Public Prosecutor, he realized that all six men were as good as convicted. Loxton, Edgley and Furnell would get a spell away from their fellows for the smuggling. The other three would also leave their customary haunts, in their case never to return.

Though French hated that part of the work, he was well content. "You know, Rollo," he told the young man with an approving smile, "you're a lazy devil. You should have done all that on your own. Next time you'll be thrown in and left to sink or swim as best you can."

Rollo, realizing what the last phrase involved, was content too.

Freeman Wills Crofts

The Box Office Murders

A girl employed in the box office of a London cinema falls into the power of a mysterious trio of crooks. A helpful solicitor sends her to Scotland Yard. There she tells Inspector French the story of the Purple Sickle. Her body is found floating in Southampton Water the next day. French discovers that similar murders have taken place. After gathering evidence he learns the trio's secret and runs them to ground.

The Hog's Back Mystery

The Hog's Back is a ridge in Surrey and the setting for the disappearance of several locals. A doctor vanishes, followed by a nurse with whom he was acquainted, then a third person. Inspector French deduces murder, but there are no bodies. Eventually he is able to prove his theory and show that a fourth murder has been committed.

'As pretty a piece of work as Inspector French has done…on the level of Mr Crofts' very best; which is saying something.'

E C Bentley in the *Daily Telegraph*

Freeman Wills Crofts

Inspector French's Greatest Case

We are here introduced for the first time to the famous Inspector French. A head clerk's corpse is discovered beside the empty safe of a Hatton Garden diamond merchant. There are many suspects and many false clues to be followed before French is able to solve the crime.

Man Overboard!

In the course of a ship's passage from Belfast to Liverpool a man disappears. His body is picked up by Irish fishermen. Although the coroner's verdict is suicide, murder is suspected. Inspector French co-operates with Superintendent Rainey and Sergeant M'Clung once more to determine the truth.

Freeman Wills Crofts

Mystery in the Channel

The cross-channel steamer *Chichester* stops half way to France. A motionless yacht lies in her path. When a party clambers aboard they find a trail of blood and two dead men. Chief Constable Turnbill has to call on Inspector French for help in solving the mystery of the *Nymph*.

Mystery on Southampton Water

The Joymount Rapid Hardening Cement Manufacturing Company is in serious financial trouble. Two young company employees hatch a plot to break in to a rival works, Chayle on the Isle of Wight, to find out Chayle's secret for underselling them. But the scheme does not go according to plan. The death of the night watchman, theft and fire are the result. Inspector French is brought in to solve the mystery.

OTHER TITLES BY FREEMAN WILLS CROFTS AVAILABLE DIRECT FROM HOUSE OF STRATUS

Quantity		£	$(US)	$(CAN)	€
☐	The 12.30 From Croydon	6.99	11.50	15.99	11.50
☐	The Affair at Little Wokeham	6.99	11.50	15.99	11.50
☐	Antidote to Venom	6.99	11.50	15.99	11.50
☐	The Box Office Murders	6.99	11.50	15.99	11.50
☐	The Cask	6.99	11.50	15.99	11.50
☐	Crime at Guildford	6.99	11.50	15.99	11.50
☐	Death of a Train	6.99	11.50	15.99	11.50
☐	Death on the Way	6.99	11.50	15.99	11.50
☐	Enemy Unseen	6.99	11.50	15.99	11.50
☐	The End of Andrew Harrison	6.99	11.50	15.99	11.50
☐	Fatal Venture	6.99	11.50	15.99	11.50
☐	Fear Comes to Chalfont	6.99	11.50	15.99	11.50
☐	Found Floating	6.99	11.50	15.99	11.50
☐	French Strikes Oil	6.99	11.50	15.99	11.50
☐	Golden Ashes	6.99	11.50	15.99	11.50
☐	The Groote Park Murder	6.99	11.50	15.99	11.50
☐	The Hog's Back Mystery	6.99	11.50	15.99	11.50
☐	Inspector French and the Cheyne Mystery	6.99	11.50	15.99	11.50

ALL HOUSE OF STRATUS BOOKS ARE AVAILABLE FROM GOOD BOOKSHOPS OR DIRECT FROM THE PUBLISHER:

Internet: www.houseofstratus.com including author interviews, reviews, features.

Email: sales@houseofstratus.com please quote author, title and credit card details.

OTHER TITLES BY FREEMAN WILLS CROFTS AVAILABLE DIRECT FROM HOUSE OF STRATUS

Quantity		£	$(US)	$(CAN)	€
☐	Inspector French and the Starvel Tragedy	6.99	11.50	15.99	11.50
☐	Inspector French's Greatest Case	6.99	11.50	15.99	11.50
☐	James Tarrant, Adventurer	6.99	11.50	15.99	11.50
☐	A Losing Game	6.99	11.50	15.99	11.50
☐	Man Overboard!	6.99	11.50	15.99	11.50
☐	Many a Slip	6.99	11.50	15.99	11.50
☐	Mystery in the Channel	6.99	11.50	15.99	11.50
☐	Murderers Make Mistakes	6.99	11.50	15.99	11.50
☐	Mystery of the Sleeping Car Express	6.99	11.50	15.99	11.50
☐	Mystery on Southampton Water	6.99	11.50	15.99	11.50
☐	The Pit-Prop Syndicate	6.99	11.50	15.99	11.50
☐	The Ponson Case	6.99	11.50	15.99	11.50
☐	The Sea Mystery	6.99	11.50	15.99	11.50
☐	Silence for the Murderer	6.99	11.50	15.99	11.50
☐	Sir John Magill's Last Journey	6.99	11.50	15.99	11.50
☐	Sudden Death	6.99	11.50	15.99	11.50

ALL HOUSE OF STRATUS BOOKS ARE AVAILABLE FROM GOOD BOOKSHOPS OR DIRECT FROM THE PUBLISHER:

Hotline: UK ONLY: **0800 169 1780**, please quote author, title and credit card details.
INTERNATIONAL: **+44 (0) 20 7494 6400**, please quote author, title, and credit card details.

Send to: **House of Stratus**
24c Old Burlington Street
London
W1X 1RL
UK

Please allow following carriage costs per ORDER
(For goods up to free carriage limits shown)

	£(Sterling)	$(US)	$(CAN)	€(Euros)
UK	1.95	3.20	4.29	3.00
Europe	2.95	4.99	6.49	5.00
North America	2.95	4.99	6.49	5.00
Rest of World	2.95	5.99	7.75	6.00
Free carriage for goods value over:	50	75	100	75

PLEASE SEND CHEQUE, POSTAL ORDER (STERLING ONLY), EUROCHEQUE, OR INTERNATIONAL MONEY ORDER (PLEASE CIRCLE METHOD OF PAYMENT YOU WISH TO USE)
MAKE PAYABLE TO: STRATUS HOLDINGS plc

Order total including postage:_____Please tick currency you wish to use and add total amount of order:

☐ £ (Sterling)   ☐ $ (US)   ☐ $ (CAN)   ☐ € (EUROS)

VISA, MASTERCARD, SWITCH, AMEX, SOLO, JCB:
☐☐☐☐☐☐☐☐☐☐☐☐☐☐☐☐☐☐☐☐☐☐☐☐

Issue number (Switch only):
☐☐☐

Start Date: **Expiry Date:**
☐☐/☐☐   ☐☐/☐☐

Signature: _____

NAME: _____

ADDRESS: _____

_____

POSTCODE: _____

Please allow 28 days for delivery.

Prices subject to change without notice.
Please tick box if you do not wish to receive any additional information. ☐

House of Stratus publishes many other titles in this genre; please check our website (**www.houseofstratus.com**) for more details